HEALED BEGINNINGS

DIANA DERICCI

Purple Sword Publications
Tucson, AZ

HEALED BEGINNINGS
Copyright © 2015 DIANA DERICCI
ISBN 978-1-61292-142-6
ISBN 10: 1612921426
Cover Art Designed by Anastasia Rabiyah
Edited by Sandra Sookoo and Traci Markou

Published by Purple Sword Publications, LLC
Tucson, Arizona, USA
www.PurpleSword.com

The Silo Series
Reading List:

Run with the Moon
Healed Beginnings
The Winter Moon's Wolf

Dedication:

For our active and veteran military, first responders, men and women, and the canine companions who serve at their side.
Thank you.

,

Chapter One

Ed Norwood propped himself on bent elbows on the grassy lakeshore, watching Jamie and Chris roughhouse like a couple of kids in the cool water. Sunshine beat down on them from a cloudless August sky. Sunglasses helped with a lot of the light, but it was still ridiculously bright with glare on ripples of water. Not enough to make him regret being there. It was a good day to do nothing at the lake.

Friends to share it along with a cooler full of drinks and barbecue waiting to be devoured. He sighed, taking a good stretch on top of it all.

Well, almost all of it was great. He loved his friends, but it was impossible to not feel like a third wheel sometimes to their antics. It was hard seeing Chris with someone else, but he had to agree, in their case, friends was much better than lovers. And as much as he wished he could be with Chris, he could see how much Jamie adored Chris. Saying Jamie hung the moon for Ed's ex was a world-class understatement.

Ed knew jealousy played a big part in it. The two of them were so perfect for each other, in ways Ed had yet to find for himself. Chris was all chest—broad and strong. Jamie was like a reed, a runner if Ed had ever seen one, and Ed had seen Jamie's sprint. The guy could outrun a speeding train…almost. Jamie also had Chris smiling all the time. It was simply one of those truths. Ed would never regret losing Chris if he was this happy.

Ed couldn't say he had been as lucky since they'd gone their separate ways.

Sadly, there really weren't a lot of choices in Silo for a gay guy. He was glad he had friends, but some days... He blew out a breath, wishing.

Regardless of his own angst-filled emotions, he didn't fight the smile when Chris hefted Jamie and tossed him like a sack of rocks to make a big splash, Jamie squealing the whole way.

Chris yelped and tried to backpedal right after. There was a misstep, a flailing of arms, and then he went underwater as well. A heartbeat later, Jamie popped out of the water waving a pair of red swim trunks.

"Ha!" Jamie cheered, then he dove for the bank in Ed's direction.

Chris' arms broke the water and he stood, laughing through his glares. "Jamie! Give those back!"

An evil grin was all Ed saw. Then the trunks were launched in his direction. They landed with a soggy plop at the lip of the water.

"Ed, help me out, man!" Chris had stopped in waist-deep water because Jamie was already out of reach in the shallower water. Chris' trunks were a yard or two away from where he lay on a towel on the grass.

"Don't do it, Ed!" Jamie cried, gasping and laughing as he plowed through the water, getting closer inland and out of reach. "You saw what he did!"

"Uh, Jamie, you don't weigh more than a wet napkin." Ed chuckled when Jamie grumbled. "And you and I both know he'll do it again."

The sparkle in Jamie's eyes proved he knew this.

"Are you really going to leave him stranded out there?" Ed asked Jamie as he came nearer and dropped to the ground beside him.

"Not for long." Jamie propped his chin on a braced hand to gaze right at Ed, effectively ignoring his boyfriend who stood buck naked in the water. "He'll forgive me." Then he winked.

Ed didn't want to know how or who would be doing the forgiving. He drifted to his back, closing his eyes. "Don't remind me." Hell, he couldn't remember the last time he'd gotten laid.

Jamie nudged him with a knee. "You'll find yours. You will."

"Jamie!"

Ed opened his eyes to see Jamie blinking in full-blown, faked innocence when he faced the water.

"Yes?"

"You are going to be in so much trouble," Chris threatened with a menacing growl.

Jamie laughed. "He's all bark." He rolled his eyes. "Fine! Say you're sorry for tossing me like a sock."

Chris swayed in the water, pacing most likely. Ed didn't doubt he probably wanted to throttle the guy next to him. Chris glared once and then heaved a huge sigh. Ed swore he felt the breeze from twenty feet away.

"I'm sorry."

Jamie glanced to Ed. "Did that sound like he meant it to you?"

Ed shrugged. It sounded legit to him. Legitimately fake, but he wasn't going to point that out. He was sure Jamie knew what he was getting into with Chris. Ed was equally sure Chris wouldn't so much as tug a hair on Jamie's body in reprimand.

"I stand by what I've said before. You two are sickening when it comes to cute."

Jamie chortled quietly. Then he fell silent and gave Ed the most unsettling look. "Something's telling me your time is coming."

"You're just being optimistic so I don't look like a total loser hanging out with you guys."

Jamie tilted his neck and gave Ed an unfazed look. "No, I really don't think so."

"Jamie!"

Jamie startled. "Oh! Right. You're naked."

That reply earned him fists planted on hips. "No, duh. You did it."

Jamie gave his lover the largest shit-eating grin Ed had ever seen. "I sure did, didn't I?" he purred. Then he stood and bent to scoop up the aforementioned swim trunks. "You mean these?" He dangled them daringly from a finger. Ed rose up to watch the outcome.

"You do know there are other people here. Kids," Chris pointed out.

"Waaay over by the boat docks. I wouldn't do that to you with an audience."

Ed made an impatient raspberry. *Guess I don't count.*

Jamie twisted to catch his gaze over a shoulder. "Best friends excluded. Not like you haven't seen it all already."

Ed's jaw actually loosened. "You're okay with that?"

Jamie contemplated the question for a few seconds. "That you've seen all of Chris? Can't change his past. That you get to see him now? That lake would have to be on fire before he'd come another two inches closer."

"Huh," Ed grunted. Jamie knew him pretty damned well. The both of them.

"I also know that looking is all anyone else would get the opportunity to do, and it would have to be one of fastest stolen glances in history. I don't question that about him in the least."

"You trust him that much?"

"With my life," Jamie said evenly. He faced the lake and a watchful Chris. "All right. I'm coming." He waded into the water, holding the treasured trunks in a tight hand.

Ed waited for the traditional grab-and-dunk, but instead got to watch one of the hottest kisses ever.

He groaned and sank to the ground, ignoring them both.

* * * *

Ed dropped his duffle on the bed, opening it to empty. He sniffed the shirt and tossed it in the dirty clothes hamper. It smelled like the barbecue pit and sauce. He slipped from his sandals with swim trunks being flung in the direction of the bathroom to hang to dry. The clothes he wore plus the rest of his things from his day at the lake followed, and then he flopped onto the bed naked. He needed to shower, but wasn't in a hurry.

He'd had a good day, fun, sun, and friends. What could be better? He slanted a crooked arm over his face and heaved a dejected breath. He knew how it could be better, but unfortunately it wasn't happening. His day to day was beginning to feel like he was spinning his wheels, getting nowhere and doing nothing. Maybe he should move back home.

He'd signed on to the fire department about four years ago, and for the most part, he'd been happy in Silo. It was quiet, a small town with possibilities. The town was progressive even for being nowhere. Then he'd met Chris and…wow. He was amazing. Knocked Ed right on his ass, literally. They'd bumped into each other on the sidewalk outside of Mabel's and to apologize, Chris had bought him lunch. They'd dated for a while. He'd hoped they'd last longer, make a deeper commitment, but it wasn't meant to be. It had been a mutual split. There was something missing, and they both knew it. The sex had been great, though. Now, Chris was officially off the available list. He was so taken he might as well be married.

Ed couldn't even hate Jamie. Better to be friends with both than neither. It wasn't all that hard being around them, except for moments like today when it was all too clear to Ed that being alone sucked ass.

Getting a grip on the wallowing self-pitying he was doing, he stood and ambled to the bathroom to clean up. He was back on shift the next morning. He was lucky to be one of the staffed firemen on the department's roster. The city paid for a team of ten for each of their two locations, with another twenty-five who were volunteer. The staffed firefighters worked in four day shifts, with three off, which meant there were enough bodies to overlap hours. They were expected to always have someone available for emergencies. The staffed men also were required to stay on top of all their training and credentials. If something big happened, everyone who was trained and available throughout Silo was known to show up. Several in town had trained skills, but most days it was quiet and the base crew onboard could handle the calls.

Heck, fires at the vet clinic were practically the only rolling calls they had all summer. Not exactly a mecca of adventure. What it amounted to was, being single, he could live on the abysmal pay the city allotted for the career crew. Too many had families and children to raise, so they had to work and volunteer. But being a firefighter was something Ed wanted to do, what he'd been training for since midway through his sophomore year of high school.

He tested the water flow in the shower and then stepped beneath it, cutting off the outside world by tugging the curtain closed in the cramped half-shower. His living quarters were a small rental about halfway between Silo and Stiller Springs, what had likely been a detached garage but had been refurbished for one of the previous generation's kids. It had a single front room where the living room and kitchen were, but there really wasn't a dining area for a table. He usually propped a table in front of the TV if he felt like he needed one. The bedroom was barely large enough for a double bed and a single dresser, and the one bathroom was tiny, but it was only him and so long as he had hot water, he didn't care. It didn't require a lot of upkeep and most of the week he was at the fire station anyway. Aside from that, all he had to do was carry his laundry to the main house. Pauline, the owner, had sliced off the washroom and had given him a key to that door. It wasn't a bad setup as far as bachelor pads went.

There were two new apartment complexes in the works closer to Silo. Probably considerably nicer than the few hundred feet he called home, but he knew the rent would be more than he could afford on the town's salary pay.

If he worked in a larger community, he'd more than likely make far better money than in Silo but he also knew how hard it was to get into those stations. There were usually waiting lists just to test and interview.

When he blew out an agitated breath, water scattered wildly. He closed his eyes to tip into the shower stream, attempting to release the restlessness haunting him. Clean and rinsed, he turned off the water and opened the hanging curtain. Grasping a towel, he dried off and tied it around his waist.

He finished dressing, considering a snack since he still had a couple of hours before he'd have to think about going to sleep. Opening the refrigerator to investigate, he closed it a disgusted moment later, standing and gazing around the small apartment hopefully, yet knowing it was fruitless. He was still restless and craving.

He really didn't know for what.

Chapter Two

Duncan Nichols threw the Frisbee for Margo, watched her gallop then gracefully launch and arch midair to snag it in her jaws. She trotted back as though she'd earned a medal. Her tail whipped like a dervish, wagging her butt as much as she was wagging her tail.

"Good one, girl," Duncan praised her with a rub on the head when she released the disc for him. He cocked his arm and let it sail. She spun and tore over the grass in the park. Her form bowed as she snagged the Frisbee out of the air. This was the best kind of fun for her, and honestly, it got Duncan out of the house. It got him away from his computer and out in the sunshine.

He carried the Frisbee after her last jump and walked over to the table where his backpack waited to straddle the concrete bench seat. He slid the zipper open on the pack, rooting around for his water bottle. After taking a couple good swallows, he put some in a travel bowl for Margo and let her quench her thirst too. When she licked it clean, he added a little more and leisurely sipped on what was left in the bottle.

He caught the gaze of a young woman as she jogged past. When she saw him taking care of his dog, she smiled and gave a light wave. He nodded, but didn't smile as she bounced by. Duncan didn't really want to attract a woman's interest. Propping an elbow to hold his head on his right hand, he knew better than to think a guy was going to want to suffer trying to love someone like him.

Dropping the drained bottle into his pack and closing up her bowl to do the same, he zipped it shut and slid one of the straps over a shoulder. He clipped Margo's leash on her collar and she instantly fell into step at his side. She was always so eager to please and he loved spoiling her.

Margo was the biggest reason he was even willing to participate in life. After rehab, he'd been in limbo. He wasn't in the military any longer. He was on permanent disability. A job wasn't the easiest thing under the circumstances, though placement channels helped him find something that would give him purpose. Frankly, filing insurance claims and paperwork wasn't exciting in the least, but it made life less sunrise to sundown. Then a little more than three years ago, Duncan had watched a documentary on Search and Rescue animals, and had found himself enthralled by their intelligence and dedication. He'd scoured information on the animals, breeds and training.

He was able to find entire SAR segments from 9/11, Katrina and other disasters to study the animals and listen to their handlers. Finally believing he'd found something he was meant to do, he started his hunt for the perfect match at the shelters.

He wasn't looking for a breed so much as an animal that would *click*. An animal that would grow and trust in him as he'd come to trust in their ability and growth.

Margo had been a pound puppy in every sense of the word. A stray off the streets, she looked like a mix of Labrador and some breed of shepherd. Big brown eyes, paws the size of tangerines and an immediate want to crawl all over Duncan. With a clean bill of health and a leash, he'd brought that bundle of energy home.

Training started that day. Between crate training, house breaking, leashes and all the other necessities that came with a canine companion, he very quickly became the center of her world. After giving her a couple of days to settle into her new home and to bond with him, he started the ground work for her SAR training.

She was an eager learner and loved her Frisbee. Duncan had trained her specifically for air scenting, where she could track on broad scents in the wind and on the ground rather than a trail of specific scent. She knew when he put on her SAR harness, she was going to do something very special.

He unlocked the front door on his side of the duplex, letting her dash inside after he'd released her and given permission to relax. She went right to her water to slurp and gulp loudly then, with a wide swinging tongue, she panted, waiting for her next cue.

"Go lay down, Margo," he said. "Dad has to get some more work in today."

She wagged her tail and trotted to her bed in the corner of the living room, curling up to rest.

He cleaned out the backpack and hung it in the closet. Slipping off his sneakers, he curled his toes to stretch and sauntered to the second bedroom of the half-sized home, where his computer and other office things were.

It was sometime later when he straightened and noticed the hour. It took time to type with only his right hand. He could use the prosthetic on his left for quite a bit, but not on something requiring as much finesse as typing.

After closing the files he had open, he sent his time report and called it done for the day.

Dinner was easy and light. Then it was some TV and a beer until his eyelids grew heavy. When he stood, Margo trailed him and he let her out for the last potty break while he got ready for bed. By the time he was finished, so was she and she joined him in the bedroom. She automatically walked into her crate and got comfortable, her big, brown gaze following him until he was in bed and tugging the blankets up around himself to settle for the night. A canine huffed sigh and groan made him smile.

Her *it's about time* sounds. Humans were fussy and took way too long to tuck up and fall asleep. He watched as her eyes closed now that he was in bed. It always gave him a warm sensation in his chest knowing she was watching over him as much as he did for her.

* * * *

The ringing phone dragged Duncan mercilessly from a deep sleep. He muttered as he shifted, reaching with a heavy limb for the beast on the bedside table. "Hello?"

"Nichols?"

"Yeah," he tried, though it was dry and kind of croaky.

"How quick can you and your dog get to the Silo area? We've had major touchdowns in Silo and Stiller Springs and there's reports of people missing."

Duncan scrubbed down his face, trying to place the towns on his mental map. "That's southwest from here, right?"

"Yes."

He nodded. He knew the area. "Let me get up and moving. I can be there in a few hours."

"I'll add your team to the aid list and let the search teams on the ground know you're on your way."

"Thanks." He hung up and shifted to sit on the edge of the bed.

Margo was watching expectantly. Daddy getting up in the middle of the night wasn't normal. Daddy getting up with an air of purpose was even rarer.

"C'mon girl. Going to work."

She waddled out of the crate and sat at his feet, her tail sweeping the floor in restrained anticipation. She knew this wasn't a drill. He smiled, glad at least one of them could function on a mere few hours of sleep.

He quickly readied himself and packed his gear and Margo's. Loading up into the Ridgeline, he made sure she was safe in her travel crate and belted down on the back seat then turned on the GPS and set the route.

Rain began to pelt him within the first hour and fierce winds battered his truck in giant gusts. There had been a time when he'd watched for bad weather, but quickly learned that wasn't going to make anything happen to put him, Margo, or their training to use any quicker. Since their registration and certification, he'd been on several searches. She was damned good and he knew they could make a difference, if it was meant to be. They didn't always make a live recovery, and that was one of the hardest situations because even if he was gutted, Margo had still succeeded by doing her best and finding their targets.

He had to slow down as the wind seemed to slice across the highway with the directness of a scythe. In several places, debris had been scattered like tossed toys. Trees had been uprooted and fencing was nothing but bundles of wire or splintered wood that had once been poles. A path of destruction literally knifed right over the highway from one side to the other. If this was only one contact, he knew he was in for a long morning.

The sun was cracking the horizon when the GPS said he was getting close. He'd checked in with his home dispatcher and Duncan had been given his first call location. He reached for the cell phone and dialed the number he'd been given earlier.

"Silo Emergency. What's your emergency?"

"This is Duncan Nichols of Independent S and R. Terry Leeson should have you expecting my team."

"Oh, thank God." The young woman's voice instantly lost her prim professionalism. "Yes, Mr. Nichols! Please come to the Silo Fire Department. We're doing an emergency meeting in less than an hour to start looking for folks. We've already got five missing reports."

"Give me your exact address location." He entered it into the GPS as she did. "I have it. Barring road blockage, I can be there within the half hour."

"I'll let them know. Thank you!"

She disconnected and he slipped the phone into the nearest cup holder. Rain still battered his truck in torrents. Watching those rivers of water, he wasn't sure they were out of the woods yet.

Arriving at the well-lit station, he parked in the mass of vehicles, everything from pickup trucks to Jeeps to little cars. People gathered inside the emergency bay and talked in lowered tones. Several were in uniform or VFD T-shirts. Hardly anyone was bone dry. Pulling his windbreaker with the bright red-and-blue ISAR logo on it together to zip it closed, he slid his left hand into the pocket and left it there.

A sharp whistle cut through all the noise in an instant. "Let's get this organized." A bulky black man with a clipboard was addressing the crowd. When their gazes met, Duncan nodded and the other man copied him, a hint of welcome and thankfulness the most he could grant Duncan in that moment.

"We have several homes and trailers damaged or destroyed. Gas is working as fast as they can on capping the lines. Once that is done, they'll let us out to begin searching. I have a list of seven who are already being reported as missing by family members or neighbors."

Duncan caught that. The count had gone up by two.

"There's another storm cell bearing down on us and we only have a short window to see if we can find any of these people before that breaks open and causes flooding. I'm going to divide up the territory. SAR, I want you to go with Norwood." He pointed with the end of his pen toward a tall, kind of thick guy standing with crossed arms and a grim look on his features.

Duncan met his gaze and nodded. They'd do pleasantries later. He listened as directions were given and as much detail as they had followed that. When the crowd started to disperse, he walked up to the organizer and offered his hand.

"Duncan Nichols."

"Terry Leeson. Thanks for coming." He swept a glance over Duncan's shoulder. "You ready, Ed?"

"Yeah," came the grunt.

The man Duncan had spoken to came to his side. "Ed, this is the SAR team that was called in. Take him up to Old Holly Road first. Let's hope that baby girl can be found."

Duncan gulped. *A baby?* "How young?"

"Three," Terry said. He studied the gripped clipboard in his unsteady hands, obviously fighting to keep his control and composure. He straightened a moment later, saying, "I know the family and Ashley is going crazy."

Duncan firmed his jaw. He faced Ed. "You know where?"

"Yeah. The biggest funnel ripped right through about four this morning. Caught us all off our guard. There were four touchdowns."

Duncan hissed. "Okay. Let's go find her."

Chapter Three

Ed was shaken, and considering what he did, what he faced, and how much he trained when he wasn't doing anything else, that was saying something. The alarms had gone off in town but the outskirts, he later learned, had already been hit and hard. Phone line communication was hit or miss, and two cell towers had been knocked offline. It was making things difficult to reconnect family and neighbors.

Weather like last night's was random and so unpredictable. Rain storms came and went, but tornadoes? At night? He'd been asleep in his bunk upstairs when the first alarms went off. Worry was high that more would be missing or had been killed because of when they'd hit. The heat this summer had been insane and it hadn't been nearly cool enough at night.

Ed walked next to the guy they'd called in to help with the searching. He was Ed's height, narrow but not exactly wiry, and seemed fit. By the scruff on his chin, he'd been pulled out of bed as well. He didn't seem inclined to talk much as he approached a blue truck. He grabbed a pack off the front seat, then opened the rear door. Ed spotted the crate and the dog inside.

"Margo, present." The dog stepped forward and lowered her head. The collar of the harness went over her head and she twisted her body to allow room to find the buckle ends. Ed watched as the SAR guy buckled her up.

The wind had died down to an eerie stillness, moisture and the smell of wet everything heavy in the air. Her handler leaned and pressed their heads together, murmuring words. A tail wag followed.

"Okay, Margo, time to work. Heel." She leaped from the truck and went to the guy's side. "Ready when you are."

"Doesn't she need a leash?"

"Sometimes."

Ed had expected more than a one word answer, but when it didn't look like more was coming, he spun and headed for his Jeep.

He climbed behind the wheel. The dog's handler patted the rear of the Jeep and Margo bounded in, sat, and didn't move. Turning over the motor, he said, "I missed your name."

"Duncan." He snapped his seat belt and gazed forward.

Another one word answer. Great.

Putting the vehicle in reverse, he pulled away from the station for Old Holly Road.

Watchful of debris and road damage, Ed made good time. He knew the area. There was a trailer park on Old Holly Road, working people trying to make ends meet.

It wasn't hard to see the path the twister had cut through the landscape as they got closer. Trees were either snapped in two or had limbs sheared off to the trunk. The ground looked like it had been chewed and spit back out. Even more disturbing were the blank lots where homes had once stood. A deck remained unscathed, but the house it had been attached to was completely gone. There were several cars left behind, two unfortunately pinned beneath some of those toppled trees. He prayed to a God he didn't really believe in that everyone had even a few seconds to get out alive.

"Do you know the little girl's name?"

The guy had been so quiet, the question surprised him. "Penny. I'll take you to their home lot. There might be something there to catch her scent from."

Duncan nodded, his gaze locked on the destruction as they crawled past.

"How was she missed?"

"Her father went to her room and when he saw the empty bed, thought his wife had her already and ran for it. Penny must have been hiding somewhere in her room when it started."

"They're all safe?"

"I think so. Terry has a better tab on the residents."

Conversation ceased when he rolled to a stop in front of one of the lots. The home before them looked like a giant toddler had lifted it and threw it to the ground. One end was crumpled and it had been bent in the middle. These weren't little RV-sized homes, but sturdy, landlocked mobile homes. Not as safe as a brick or even a foundation home, but the few tin cans that had been in the park were nowhere to be seen. Heavy cloud cover and the threat of more rain gave everything a somber and dilapidated aura. Absolute silence wasn't alleviating any of that either.

Duncan slid from his seat and with a motion, stayed Margo in the Jeep. He cautiously studied the ground and debris. He gazed at the treetops and then into the distance, following the path of destruction as it seemed to vanish, a wall of normal quickly appearing where it looked like the tornado had simply died.

He whistled and Margo jumped to the ground, loping to his side. She watched him like a hawk, all but glued to his leg. "Find, Margo." He pointed and the dog leaped into action scrambling around the home with her nose to the ground. "Find her, girl."

Ed went in a different direction, looking for signs of blood, or torn clothing, something that might give a hint to a child being dragged or tossed by the wind. He hoped he didn't find those first.

He caught wisps of sound as Duncan kept Margo searching. When there wasn't a sign of the child still being in the home, Ed began to worry. That meant she could be anywhere. The violent energy of a tornado could throw objects from yards to half a mile or further if it was carried in the maelstrom of the funnel. Ed knew two of the funnels had been F5 in strength. It wasn't a record breaking night, but came damn close.

"Ed." It wasn't a loud call, but it whipped him around to Duncan instantly. He jogged over.

Together, they caught up to the dog pacing around a jumble of what must have been a wood structure and at one time, an above ground pool.

"Find, Margo," Duncan directed, and they watched as she began to intensify her snooping, pawing at debris. "Off, Margo." She immediately backed up.

"Let me get my travel board and EMT kit." Ed's heart was in his throat that if Penny was under there, he wouldn't have a need for either.

Duncan nodded, carefully starting to dig into the pile of broken boards. Ed sprinted for the rear of his

Jeep, and rejoined them, helping Duncan draw pieces out of the way.

"Hold on." Ed tested a large section of nailed wood. Bracing it with his palms, he rose to a knee. "See anything that will collapse?"

"No. I see more of the pool wall."

With a heave and a thrust, he toppled the floor of what had once been the pool deck to the side. The crack of dried wood splintering in a thousand places was loud in the remaining quiet. Then Ed heard, "I see her!" He watched Duncan scramble under the pool and crawl up to her. The sound of relief was clear in that expectant silence. "She's alive. Slide me the board."

Ed pushed it in Duncan's direction until it was taken out of his reach. He couldn't believe they'd located Penny, and so quickly. He looked over his shoulder, and found a patiently attentive and watchful pooch. "Good girl, Margo." She panted and slapped her tail on the ground where she obediently waited.

"She's amazing," Ed heard Duncan say. "That girl has a nose better than a rat. Do you have phone service?"

Ed withdrew his cell phone and growled. "Not yet."

"She's beat up, respirations are a little fast. No breaks but she's got a good sized knot on her forehead."

"We'll take her to the first responder location if I can't get a relay."

He scooted out of the way as Duncan inched the board forward to Ed. With as smooth a motion as possible, he brought her out into the overcast daylight.

After double checking all the tension straps, he added the C-collar to transport her.

Duncan flexed his right hand. "Let me get a good grip. You need to go backward."

Ed reached for the board handles and together they rose to their feet, steadying the little girl between them. Once Ed saw Duncan had both hands positioned, he began walking.

"Margo, heel."

She popped up and joined them.

"To your right," Duncan directed him. Ed slipped peeks over his shoulder until they were at the Jeep.

"Let's get her strapped down and I'll do quick vitals," Ed said.

Duncan helped him heft the board, and with a speed that took Ed by surprise, Duncan had it stabilized with the Jeep's installed ratchet straps. Then he slid his left hand back into his jacket pocket.

Ed realized Duncan had a glove on that hand he hadn't noticed before then. "Did you hurt yourself?"

"No. It's nothing important." A cloud flew over Duncan's features but it quickly vanished as they worked together on Penny.

Her pajamas were in bad shape, but otherwise, she wasn't, and Ed gave another silent thank you.

Duncan hopped into the pinched space behind Ed's seat, keeping a hand on the backboard. "Margo, front."

The dog cleared the door with a leap, landed on the seat and promptly hopped to the floorboard. She rested her head on the seat edge, then slid down to curl up.

"She's so well-trained." Ed started the Jeep and switched on the emergency radio.

"She also does amateur obstacle course competitions." The pride in Duncan's voice was unmistakable.

Ed reached for the radio mike, shaking his head. He wasn't sure amazing was nearly strong enough to describe what he'd seen Margo do that morning.

Ed alerted Terry they'd found Penny, and her condition. "Ten-four, on way to meet Engine Three for relay. You okay back there?" he asked Duncan. He clipped the radio mike in place beneath the dash.

"Been in worse. We're fine."

The brusque answer seemed to be the best Ed was going to get.

The drive to their meeting point was slow going to not jar the child in the back. When they reached the crossroads, he spotted Engine Three, their ambulance, rolling up over the next hill.

Ed met Adam at the Jeep as Susan opened the rig. "How is she?" Adam asked.

"Her color is okay. Her breathing is still a little fast, but she doesn't have any open bleeding." Adam wrote it all down on the chart where they'd add their own vitals.

"Okay, let's get Miss Penny onboard. Her parents are already on their way to the hospital."

Duncan slipped out of the way, dropping to the ground. He opened the passenger door. Ed caught it out of the corner of his eye as he popped open a bowl and quickly gave Margo a drink.

"Who else is still MIA?"

"We had two show up, so we've only got four to go. There's a chance it's only two. Terry is trying to confirm if the Richlands are out of the area, vacation or something."

He waited as Susan and Adam transferred Penny to the gurney to travel to Stiller Springs.

"Bring the collar back to the station."

"Will do." He smacked the doors shut, leaving Susan in the rear with the little girl. Striding to the front to get behind the wheel, he pulled away, lumbering up to speed with lights snapping and flashing.

Running a hand over his hair, he turned with the empty board in hand to go back to the station himself.

Chapter Four

The next wave of rain was dropping in drenching sheets by the time they reached the firehouse. Margo wasn't happy about being under the flimsy snap-on top Ed had put into place right before he started driving, and she was letting Duncan know it by propping her chin on his shoulder and whining softly.

"I know. I won't let you melt," he chided lovingly. He reached and gave her a kind head scratch.

"Not fond of rain, huh?"

"These really vicious storms get to her."

"You're welcome to wait them out at the fire station. I'm sure Terry's going to want a full report anyway."

Duncan had expected as much. He had a report of his own to write up. "Thanks." It would be nice to stay close to dry.

"Not much for talking, are you?"

Duncan's lips twitched, then he said, "No."

Ed chuckled quietly. He pulled up as close as he could to the building. The large bays were closed against the driving rain, but the personnel door was only a couple of yards away. Duncan guessed it was as good as he was going to get.

With his pack over a shoulder, he opened the Jeep door and called for Margo. She bounded out in a furry blur. He smacked the door shut, and they both raced for the dry safety the doorway offered.

He shook his head much the same as she shook her body once they were inside.

"Stay in the halls!"

"Okay!" Ed shouted back. He shrugged for Duncan.

One of the guys brought them towels and they dried off in the hallway instead of slogging all the water and muck into the station.

Duncan set his supply pack against the wall and unclipped Margo's rescue harness. "Off duty, girl," he said. He got a lick across the face for it. "Yeah, yeah." But he was grinning.

Feeling the weight of a stare, he twisted and caught Ed watching him with Margo. Ed blinked then looked the other way hurriedly.

Duncan hadn't really given it much thought, but the guy was better than good looking. Brown hair and a bold jaw, broad but soft looking lips, if a little thin, and to make him even that much more masculine, he had a small cleft in his chin. There wasn't a lot hidden beneath a soaked T-shirt, and he seemed pretty solid to Duncan. He knew they were about the same height. Beyond that, he didn't even want to try to begin to guess or hope.

Just then, a cell phone rang.

Ed twitched, then yanked his out of a pocket. "Yeah? Jamie! You guys okay? Oh good. Yeah, we're okay here. Yeah, he's still here. What? Where?" Ed gazed down with a concerned expression where Duncan was still kneeling by Margo. "Did Chris already call it into the emergency center? Okay. Okay, calm down." Ed rubbed a hand over his forehead. "Hold on." He put a hand over the face of the phone. "We're not done yet. I need to get the details."

"I'm here for as long as you guys need me."

The flash of relief was intense on Ed's face. "Be right back." He jogged down the hall to vanish for a moment. Duncan leaned to rest against the wall. Margo snuggled close to curl against his chest.

* * * *

It was well after four in the afternoon before Duncan was done. After Silo, he was sent to Stiller Springs, then back to Silo. Already made to feel at home there by the crew, he went to the fire station last.

Terry was one of the first to greet him when he and Margo came in, grasping him in a strangling hug. "Penny is going to be fine. She's already awake. Nothing but mild shock and exposure."

Duncan was real glad to hear that. One of the searches in Stiller Springs hadn't ended as well. Maybe that was why he returned there. He needed the reaffirmation of the living. He'd already seen enough death in his lifetime.

Ed spotted him as soon as he hit the kitchen with Terry in the lead. "Hey guys! That's her. She's incredible."

"No way! She's gorgeous!" One of the guys sitting at the table in the room lowered a hand and Duncan put Margo off duty to play. She'd earned it and then some. "What is she?" the guy making friends asked.

"Part rat, part rabbit, Malinois and black Lab, and about five percent terrier. All ham."

The guys at the table with Ed laughed as she started scoping out head scratches and attention.

One of the crew pulled up a chair and motioned for Duncan to sit. He was dead on his feet. A hot shower, a hot meal, and a soft bed, hopefully in that order, were immediate on his list, but he could take a few minutes to spend there.

"Duncan said she also competes," Ed offered.

"Really? I love watching those shows on *Animal Planet*."

"She doesn't get air time, but she's earned some medals." Duncan couldn't hide his pride in her.

"I bet she has," Ed said at his shoulder. "Where did you train?"

"We did scent training in California with one of the K-9 academies. I did the majority of her obedience and obstacle training."

"How long have you guys been at this?" one of the others asked.

"About two years now." He propped his left hand on his thigh out of sight and rested his right on the table.

"I'd love to get some info on it." The guy giving Margo all kinds of love didn't seem to want to let her go. "Ed was telling us how she found Penny."

"Search and Rescue dogs are incredible," Duncan replied.

The guy loving on Margo stood and offered a hand across the table. "I'm Davey." The rest of them did the same, introducing themselves. Duncan shook hands, his other hand slipping into his jacket pocket without a thought.

A full plate of food appeared on the table in front of him. "Family gets fed before they leave," Terry said, a little brusque, not quite making eye contact.

At Duncan's start of surprise, a couple of the guys chuckled warmly. Davey said, "Yep, you've been adopted. Deal with it."

"You should be here on Susan's nights. That woman missed her calling." They started telling tales as Duncan dug into the plate of corned beef hash and spring vegetables that tasted fresh, right out of a garden. He laughed quietly when they told of the night Barley—his last name—set off the *in house* fire alarms by burning garlic bread. Stories of cookouts and grilling, friendly arguments over the best pasta, and good teasing over too much salt, or too little, followed. He'd missed this depth of camaraderie, missed the friendship of being with a unit.

Flashes of the men, the smells of the day he'd lost his hand, the heat and pain, bombarded him from out of nowhere and he froze. Exhaustion and all the adrenaline rushes had compounded into one giant release. His heart raced with an erratic rhythm but he wrestled it to get it under control before the panic became noticeable.

"You okay?" Ed leaned close to where Duncan had ducked his head.

"Yeah. Hiccups." It was easier to lie than to let them know what kind of a basket case he really and truly was.

"Hey, get our guy some water," Ed called and someone across the table stood. A glass appeared a minute later.

He took several slow measured swallows. "Thanks." He sucked the moisture from his lips then set the glass down.

"No problem." And Ed smiled. A relaxed smile.

His eyes are brown. And for some reason, noticing that made Duncan's heart trip all over again.

"Hey, would you be willing to bring Margo to do a demonstration?" Davey asked, with this *I have a brainstorm idea* brightness to his face. "We're getting ready to do our annual fundraiser for the station and she would be a star for the day."

"That's a great idea," Terry agreed from where he now sat at the end of the table. "If Duncan is willing, we'd be more than happy to make room for her and whatever you want to do with her."

"When is it?" Duncan asked, licking his fork one last time before putting it on his cleaned plate. Damn, that had been good. Better than the sandwich he would have managed at home.

"Labor Day weekend."

"Wow. That's only three weeks away," Duncan said. Heads around the table bobbed in agreement.

"Short notice?" Ed said next to him.

"No, we're flexible." He didn't want to horn in on their town festivals, though.

"Could you put something together in three weeks to do a couple of demonstrations for the crowds? You could even promote ISAR and the SAR programs," Terry offered.

"I can bring a couple of her transportable obstacles. I'll need a little space to set them up. The discovery demonstrations would be great to get the kids involved. We did those for her training."

"There's room on the back street. That'll be blocked off anyway." Davey had a pocket notebook out and was writing notes down now. "Need anything special?" He looked expectantly across the table.

Duncan thought about it for a second. "No, not that I can think of."

"We'll get one of the sponsors to print us a few more flyers to get the word out. We usually do all right but this will add a little more to it." Davey glanced at the dog now resting on the floor behind Duncan. "How could you not fall for that kind of face?"

"Have you seen Harris' wife?" someone muttered.

A roar of laughter followed.

"Man, that's *ruuuff,*" came a growled rejoinder.

Duncan lost it right after Ed.

Not too much later, everyone began to disperse. Ed trailed Duncan outside. "Thanks for everything you did today, Duncan."

"It's what I do."

"Long drive?"

Duncan shrugged. "About two hours, I guess." Duncan put a hand on his truck, staring at nothing, tense but well aware of what was coming. "Just spill it, Ed. You don't have to pull punches. You've been on the verge since I walked in with Terry." He opened the rear door. He knew what was coming. Didn't mean he had to like it.

Ed gave Duncan a clear gaze. "Is your hand okay? You've been favoring it all day. If you've hurt yourself, you don't have to act like you didn't around here. We'll get you patched up."

Duncan sighed and withdrew his left hand from its pocket. "I hate special treatment." He tugged his jacket sleeve upward, exposing the fake hand prosthetic.

"Oh. Okay." Ed fell silent. A thousand questions flitted over his face. His lips twitched as he bit at them.

Duncan rearranged the jacket back into place to cover the flesh tone that wasn't a match to Duncan's own skin, as well as the extended socket that covered his lower arm.

Ed stayed close while Duncan crated Margo and gave her a good head rub.

"See you in a few weeks," he said after getting behind the wheel. He didn't quite look at Ed either.

"Yeah, yeah," he stammered, stumbling over the words.

Chapter Five

Duncan pulled up behind the fire station early on Saturday morning, and when one of the guys recognized him, they moved the barricades for him to drive in and find a spot. He stood from behind the wheel, holding the door open by the window frame.

Terry came over and shook his hand. "Glad you could make it."

Duncan studied the lot and the surrounding area. They had shade tents, tossing games for the kids, an inflatable bouncy house, and more grills than a Chevy convention.

"You can set up on the grass over there." Terry pointed to a vacant area. "Do you need help?"

"No, but thanks. I have some ideas for later for getting the crowd involved and showing off Margo's skills."

"Great. Let me know what you want to do and we'll figure it all out."

He let Margo out of her crate, and she leaped to the ground at his side. To keep her out of the way, he had her jump into the bed of the truck until he was finished unloading. Piece by piece, he laid out the course equipment he'd brought. A few were Margo's favorites, a couple of the more challenging ones as well as the tunnel. She absolutely adored her tunnel.

He was setting up the stilt bridge when he felt a person at his side. A glance over his shoulder proved his suspicion right. The big fireman was hard to miss. "Hi, Ed."

"Hey," he said a little unsure, sweeping from Duncan to the layout with confusion warping his brow. "Why isn't anyone helping you?"

"Don't really need it. I do this all the time when I move her obstacles for training."

"Oh." He slid fingertips into jeans pockets.

Duncan was well aware Ed was doing his best to not look at Duncan's left hand. He wore the glove and a long sleeve shirt with his jeans. It was exactly what he hated, that *feeling*. He didn't really care if people knew he had the prosthetic. The glove made it obvious something was different. He did care if people thought he couldn't function being short five working fingers—well, four and a thumb. He snickered under his breath at the internal joke. It had taken him a long time to have the ability *to* joke about it.

"What kind of stuff were you planning?" Ed asked, feigning hanging out. Or trying to make it seem that way if Duncan were to take a guess.

"I'll have her do the course a couple of times, and I have scent decoys to give to the kids as they show up. I'll need someone to pick them out and explain the exercise. I've found Margo can pick up on my signals if I know who the target is."

"Really?"

Duncan's lips dared to twitch at the incredulity in his tone, then he focused on bracing the wood in his hand. "Yeah. I've learned she can read me like a box of dog treats."

Ed barked a laugh then stopped.

"Hey, Ed!"

Duncan looked in the direction Ed did and spotted the two guys walking up. One waved, the shorter, and yeah, if pressed, Duncan would say the cuter of the two. It took a second for Duncan to realize they were holding hands, openly.

"*Hey, good looookin'. Whatcha got cookin',*" the cuter one sang. He hip bumped Ed.

"Not me. They know better than to put me behind a grill. I put out fires, not keep them going."

The two friends laughed.

"You must be Duncan. Chris Rose. Didn't really get to say thank you for all your work when you were here."

Duncan shook his hand. "You're welcome."

"Is this the cutie who did the snoopin'?" Cute stuff lowered to the ground and made friends with Margo.

"That's her," Duncan said.

"Her name's Margo and she's the smartest dog I've ever seen."

Duncan smiled at Ed's unabashed praise.

"Oh, I'm Jamie." Cute stuff tilted his chin to gaze upward and Duncan was speared by two of the bluest eyes, ever. "Since Lug One and Two don't know how to make proper introductions."

Duncan smiled easily. "Nice to meet you, Jamie. Both of you." He caught Ed's gaze. "I take it you're Lug Two?"

"Actually, I'm Lug One, he's Furball." Ed tipped his head to Chris.

"Oh?"

Chris grinned at the teasing. "Yeah. My brothers and I run the town's vet clinic."

"Nice," Duncan said.

"We'll let you finish setting up. Can't wait to see Margo's skills." Jamie stood, giving Margo a final ear scratch. She panted but didn't move a step away from Duncan.

Duncan watched Chris and Jamie practically crawl into each other's pockets as they walked away. He glanced around to see who was paying attention, to see who was going to be the ass and toss a wrench in their happy, and couldn't have been more surprised when no one did. Instead, people shook hands with Chris and hugged on Jamie. Duncan could tell Jamie was the hugger and Chris... Chris smiled and didn't bat an eyelash.

He hadn't seen anything that unconcerned since California.

It didn't take long to finish setting up the mini-course he'd planned for Margo, extending and snaking the tunnel last. He noticed one of the day volunteers putting up corner stakes and winding a yellow caution tape around the perimeter to keep people away from the obstacles.

It was easy to tell who was who by either the VFD T-shirts or the yellow volunteer shirt. Duncan thanked him when he was all done.

"If you're finished here, there's someone who is dying to meet you and Margo."

Duncan gave the setup one last methodical once over, then with Margo's leash in hand, said, "Lead on."

Ed led Duncan and Margo around the front of the fire station where an auxiliary women's group was selling raffle tickets. One of the big red trucks was parked out on the blacktop. Kids were getting a lesson on the many apparatuses, knobs and lights.

Davey was drawing them in as he told stories. Several were giggling though they were all hanging on every word.

"He's good," Duncan told Ed.

"He loves kids. He goes once a week to the hospital in Stiller Springs to see the kids there."

"You've got a hell of a crew, Ed."

"They're a good bunch of guys." He smiled in agreement. "There's Terry."

Duncan spotted the man holding hands with a young child. He recognized her immediately. Her thick black hair was now in braids and tied into a single gather. The knot was gone from the light mocha of her skin, and she was beaming with life, practically skipping at Terry's side. She wore a cute pink sundress and sandals with matching pink flowers on the toes. Besides Penny and Terry, another couple followed, a taller black man and a sweet-smiling brunette.

Duncan went down to a knee. "Margo, sit," he said quietly. She hunkered down, watching.

"Penny, this is the man who found you after the big wind," Terry said gently.

Penny blinked bright, shy eyes at Duncan.

"Hello, Penny. Would you like to say hi to Margo?"

She nodded. He offered his gloved hand and she grasped onto it. "You can come closer. That's right." He smiled for Penny. "Margo, shake."

His dog lifted a front paw and he showed Penny how to shake hands with her. Penny's smile grew like a sunrise.

"Margo found me," she whispered.

"She sure did," Duncan said in answer, matching her smile. "Margo helped us get you back to your mom and dad." A swift peek upward showed Penny's mother with her hand over her mouth being held by her husband as her eyes sparkled with moisture. He eased Penny's hand up and let it slide over to pet Margo's head. "Do you have a dog?" he asked her.

"No. She's soft," she said with the brightness only a child could have.

"Maybe someday you can do what I do and help people." She gave him one of those guileless smiles in answer.

"Okay, Penny," her mother said. Penny scooted away to stand next to her dad. When Duncan stood up, he was tackled by the brunette. "Thank you, thank you, thank you," she choked out.

Duncan gave her a one-armed hug. "You're very welcome." He was glad to see Penny had rebounded from the excitement so quickly, but he knew kids were like that.

"This is Ashley and Demaris. Demaris is my godson," Terry said thickly.

Duncan caught Terry's gaze and recalled all the anxiety from the morning of the storms in his eyes. Knowing the ties that connected them now, Duncan completely understood his worry of that day. Duncan shook Demaris' hand.

"You treat that girl right," Demaris said, tipping his chin toward Margo. "She gave us back our angel."

"You do the same," Duncan said, winking for Penny who giggled and hid in her dad's hip.

"Does she know a lot of tricks?" Ashley asked, lowering a hand to let Margo sniff.

"No, the paw shaking is about it. Tricks are completely different from obedience or skills."

"I never looked at it that way," Ed murmured at his shoulder.

"Go enjoy the morning," Terry told them. "Ed can help you with the demonstrations. That okay with you Ed?"

"Sure."

Duncan got a quick kiss on the cheek from Ashley, then the group of four left Duncan and Ed behind.

"You know, she's half in love with you," Ed said, jokingly.

"Which? Penny or Ashley?"

Ed's brown eyes sparkled in the sunlight. "Oh, I'd say both."

Duncan and Ed chuckled gently. "She's a sweet little girl."

"And Ashley?" Ed asked, a slightly more serious undercurrent to the question.

"I don't think Demaris has anything to worry about."

"Oh?" Ed's steps faltered beside Duncan.

Duncan curled up Margo's leather leash in his hand, though he knew she wouldn't bolt or misbehave without it. It gave him the time to weigh the pros and cons of outing himself to someone he hardly knew. With friends, apparently good friends like Chris and Jamie, Duncan didn't think Ed would take it wrong if he told the man the truth.

Duncan paused at Ed's shoulder and met his questioning stare. "Women don't appeal to me," he explained, between them.

Ed leaned closer. "You're gay?"

Duncan nodded. "I was surprised to see your friends so open about it." Even seeing Ashley and Demaris together kind of took him by surprise.

"Chris' family has been in Silo for a long time. Plus, if you saw his brothers…" Ed rolled a shoulder. "He can handle himself, but one thing I've noticed about Silo over the years—they don't want exclusion of any kind."

"You're not from here?"

"No, transplant."

Duncan studied the leash, dying to ask the question burning the tip of his tongue. The world seemed to vanish, all of Duncan's attention fading to a bubble that encircled him and Ed. The more they talked, the more he suspected Ed was gay too, but he sincerely doubted Ed was the kind to be dominated. All that muscle… He couldn't help the dryness in his throat as he battled with himself and his own awareness. Duncan hadn't let himself look at Ed too deeply, hadn't allowed his interest to gain a foothold, but now, standing beside him, talking to him without the tension of the day they'd met between them, Duncan's blood was growing heated, his skin tingling with desire.

Duncan hadn't been involved with anyone since his discharge. Being around Ed was beginning to make him wish he were.

Chapter Six

Ed's heart was tripping a hectic rhythm. Oh, man. He took a casual step away from Duncan. An easy *Hey, I'm giving you space* kind of move because if he didn't, he was going to melt all over the other man.

Ed had seen Duncan at his focused best, had seen him and Margo work like a well-oiled machine, and here he was today, volunteering again to give something more to the community.

The longer he was quiet though, the more Ed noticed it. Maybe he'd poked a little too hard with the questions. He hadn't meant to be intrusive, but something had urged him to try to find out. He wished he could find out even more. One thing he had noticed was Duncan was a deliberate person, said what needed to be said and nothing more.

"Come on. I'll show you the station before it gets too crowded." Ed turned on a heel, catching Duncan doing the same at his side. Maybe changing the focus of the conversation would relax the other man again.

Not that Ed hated being his guide for the day. Duncan was spectacular in snug jeans, and sexy on top of it. He'd shaved, showing off a slightly angular jaw. Deep brown hair that rolled in waves like a slow tide reached his collar. Ed tore his curiosity away from the other man when they approached the outer door—or more, before he walked into it.

"You saw the kitchen and the main bay," Ed said. "The office is here." He unlocked the door and pushed it in. "It's locked for today because of the crowds." Duncan nodded in understanding. Ed showed off the smallish-sized weight room between the office and the kitchen. It had equipment, which was more than many stations for such a small town could claim. Then Ed took him upstairs to the small dorm where there were a dozen made bunks. "There are usually only a handful of us here on shift continuously, but if it gets hectic, the guys can crash here." He raised an arm toward the other side of the dorm. "The showers and lockers are in there."

"Nice setup." Duncan walked across the space to peek into the locker room. Ed followed the strut of those legs and the sweet, tight ass above them with an unwavering attention. Margo trotted at Duncan's heels sniffing as they passed the beds. She was probably having the time of her life.

Ed tried to keep his expression neutral when Duncan reversed his trip. Only instead of walking past him out the door, he stopped cold in front of Ed, blocking him at the wall.

Ed's heart kicked and began to race madly into his ribs after he'd spent the last ten minutes getting it to calm down.

Duncan's hazel gaze regarded him. Then Ed saw something in the man change. A tilt of his head, the sharpness of his eyes when they narrowed a fine hair. A very slight curve to his lips added heat to the mixed darkness of his pupils.

Meltdown initiated. He sagged to the painted brick wall behind him, just shy of stumbling in his need of support.

Duncan leaned close, almost chest to chest. The heat of his breath warmed Ed's lips. Pleasure and hunger battled, simmered, waiting for the match that would make him combust.

"Thank you for answering my question," Duncan said, barely a whisper by his ear.

"Q-question?"

Duncan growled low in his throat. Ed's eyelids dropped. The rush of need pulsating through his body made him dizzy.

"Yes." He teased Ed by licking beneath his ear. "And if I'm lucky, you'll tell me the rest before the end of today."

Warm lips ghosted from the side of his neck across his jaw to hover over his mouth. Ed almost screamed with needing to feel those lips pressed to his. Shivers raked his frame. He wanted to close the gap, but was frozen. He hadn't expected this from Duncan, and hadn't suspected the attraction as it burned and surged beneath his skin to be mutual. His hands splayed on the wall at his sides to hold himself upright. His legs had long since ceased to be of any support.

"Fuck me," Duncan breathed. "Impossible."

Gentle teeth nipped at his bottom lip and Ed whimpered. It felt like time stopped until Duncan released him. Ed pried his eyes open. He tried to talk, swallowed and managed, "What... What's impossible?"

"Nothing. For right now." Duncan tenderly licked the spot he'd bitten, soothing it. "This is mine now. I promise to kiss it better tonight."

"Yours? But—"

"Shh," Duncan said.

Blood rushed through his body with the heat of a thousand volcanoes. Nothing was working. Not muscles, not his arms or legs, and definitely not his brain. Gravity was the only thing on his side, and he only knew that because it was keeping him pinned to the wall.

"Breathe," Duncan advised, his voice as bewitching as any Ed had ever known. "Cannot believe how sexy you are. Never would have seen you like this working." Duncan inched closer, slipping a leg between Ed's to cover him body to body.

Caged now between the wall and Duncan's hard frame, Ed was a goner. Tight muscle beneath denim glided against his thigh with amazing friction, making him ache, turning his body into a flaming pyre of heat.

"I have to ask now, Ed, and be honest." Duncan's words were intense and rumbled.

Ed managed a sound, something to tell him it was okay.

"Are you a bottom?"

Ed shivered. The way he growled that almost had Ed sobbing. He was falling apart and Duncan hadn't even kissed him! Ed canted his hips and Duncan leaned closer, giving him a few seconds of pleasure if not relief.

"Never…" He gulped. "Never thought about it in top or bottom. Just what felt good."

"Oh, baby." Duncan moaned, pressed into Ed's neck, breathing him in. "You're going to feel good in so many ways. Sexy motherfucker. Can't believe you're gay." He kissed below Ed's ear then sucked on the earlobe.

Ed gasped. "Very gay," he croaked.

"That's *very* good," Duncan purred. He straightened enough to pierce Ed right through the eyes. "Don't worry. I will kiss that lip better. Tonight."

Ed bit his lip, right where Duncan had snagged it. The scorching heat visible in Duncan's eyes was hotter than any fire Ed had ever faced.

And he had to wait *all day* to see what Duncan was going to do next?

* * * *

Duncan had to focus to walk away from Ed. With firm steps, he went downstairs and strolled through the building throng of people to ease the strain and demanding pressure behind his zipper. The man was all kinds of incredible. There was safety in the anonymity of the moment. It wouldn't last, but he only needed a few minutes to clear his senses of the scent of Ed's warmed skin, or the taste of him. He certainly hadn't been expecting this turn of events with coming back to Silo.

They'd spent a long and exhausting day together doing the searches, and there had been no room or time to think about anything else. He'd been sent there to do a job. Today was his time.

He stopped in front of the small grandstand where a local band was playing. He replayed the moments in the dorm upstairs. Ed hadn't given any real clues until Duncan had turned around and caught him staring. He'd tried to keep it off his face, but Duncan wasn't going to let a good opportunity pass him by. He almost regretted not stealing that kiss when he had the chance. *Almost.* He knew by tonight, if Ed wasn't going insane with curiosity and need, then it had been nothing but a chance of the moment and some unbelievable hormones.

Duncan wanted to get his hand all over that muscled chest. He slid a look down to his left hand, a heart wrenching moment stealing his peace, but only a short-lived one. The largest drawback was the total loss of half of his tactile ability to touch and sense. Duncan sighed, then raised his head. A hand was a small price to pay for the lives he had saved.

When the song ended, he caught the singer's attention and waved him over. "Could you announce the Search and Rescue will do their first demonstration in about ten minutes in back?"

"You got it."

"Thanks." With that, he and Margo went to the truck to suit up.

"Still need my help?" Ed joined him beside his truck as he finished buckling up Margo. He sounded much calmer as well.

Duncan pointed to the back seat of the truck. "There's a satchel with three containers in it. Each one has a different scented ball. She's trained on two, and the third one is a decoy. Pick three kids, anyone who wants to be part of it and tell them to hide the ball. A pocket, or under their shirt. When it's time, I'll send her on a find and she'll get two of them."

"Any place in the crowd?"

"Yeah, random. And tell them Margo will do nothing to them. Make sure they aren't scared of dogs. Those tongue licks can bruise you."

Ed chuckled. "What will she do?"

"She'll paw at the ground then come back for me."

"Like she did with Penny," Ed said.

"Exactly."

"Okay. I'm off to play hide and seek."

"Loaded, man. That was so totally loaded." Duncan shook his head.

Ed's grin was pure evil. "Payback, hot stuff."

It was a good thing Ed turned to walk into the crowd. He nearly got the kiss Duncan had denied them both right then and there.

"Okay, girl. Ready to go wow 'em?" She wagged her tail. She knew something was up. He gave Margo a good head scratch and walked her to the roped off area.

She made her paces like a champ, and if dogs could laugh, she would have been when she came out of the tunnel, her whole body vibrating as she sat at Duncan's feet for her praise.

A hand signal and she hopped to sit at attention at his heel. A round of applause started and her tail went nuts. He hadn't been kidding when he'd told the fire crew she was all ham. She knew when it was work and when it was all for her.

"The next demonstration I'm going to have her do is a find drill. Three of you were asked to participate randomly with scented tennis balls. When I send her into the crowd, you don't have to do anything. Let her do her job. She'll tell me when she's found her target. This is only one type of drill for Search and Rescue." He smiled to play up the crowd, to keep Margo excited. "You ready to watch a nose work?"

A cheer filled the area.

Duncan lowered to Margo's side. He pointed into the crowd. "Find, Margo. Find."

She ran for the crowd with a definite wiggle, her nose up and down and all around. It only took her about a minute to find the first one. Duncan kept an eye on Margo, waiting for her training to kick in and settle her down.

She stopped in front of a young girl, pawed the ground then leaped backward to get Duncan's attention with a quick and quiet yap. The crowd parted and she waited in front of the girl, the way she was supposed to.

When a beaming smile from the girl proved Margo had done her job, he gathered the tennis ball and held it up. "Good Margo." He gave Margo a treat and a small prize to the young girl. "Thank you for helping."

Margo played it out again and when Duncan asked for the third ball to be shown, it was a teenage boy right on the front line. "Bacon," Duncan informed them, what should have been an easy find, if it had been what she'd been hunting for. A fresh round of applause was loud and long-lived.

Several hung around to talk and ask about the Search and Rescue animals. Duncan handed out brochures and business cards and when the crowd finally started to thin, he took a break for himself and Margo.

"Great job," Ed said, offering a bottled water.

Duncan poured a good amount in a bowl for Margo then drank down the rest. "It's actually fun doing this."

"You've won over quite a few."

That made Duncan smile. He liked this kind of workday considerably more than the alternative.

Chapter Seven

Ed found Duncan stretched out in the bed of his truck that afternoon, his head on Margo's shoulder, both dozing. They'd completed two more demonstrations and talked until Ed was sure Duncan would lose his voice. Margo hadn't missed one cue, one search. The proof of how much time Duncan spent with her was clear in her performance. That dog was *happy*.

He leaned on the truck bed wall, watching them for a minute. Relaxed and stretched out, a knee cocked to rest on the tire well, Duncan was one hot buffet in his pale blue shirt and jeans. Asleep, easy breaths pumped his chest. The gloved hand was down by his hip, his other arm was slung over his eyes to block sunlight. Ed wondered how he could sleep among the crowds and laughter. It was one of the things about Duncan that burned him with curiosity.

Like how had he started with Search and Rescue? How hard was it? How did he find Margo?

What happened to your hand?

Ed bit at his lip, lowering to rest his chin on bent arms. Duncan seemed so well-adjusted. Ed studied his own left hand and made a fist. How would he manage if he lost a hand? Probably not well, he admitted to himself. He also knew how shallow it made him sound that it could even matter in how he saw Duncan. It really didn't matter, but he couldn't help his own curiosity.

Straightening out one of those hands, he cupped the upright knee. "Hey." He gave him a light shake. "Wake up, sleeping beauty."

Duncan drew a deeper breath and groaned. "Snooze button."

Ed chuckled. "Sorry man. Time to pack up."

Duncan scrubbed fingers over his eyes and down his face. "*Urrgh*," he groaned. He hefted himself up onto his elbows, blinking, and Margo scrambled to his side. "Hey girl." He gathered her against his body when he sat straight. "How long was I out? I was trying for a couple of minutes and I zonked."

"Try an hour."

"Wow." He roughed Margo's face, her tongue lolling as she panted. "Some clock you are." She licked him broadly.

"Don't know how you could with all this going on." Ed meant the busy day they'd had, though it was calmer and quieter now.

"I've slept in much worse and a shitload louder."

"Where?"

"Afghanistan."

"Oh." Ed had guessed, but it only deepened his questions. "Which?"

Duncan scooted on his butt to the tailgate of the truck. "Army. Emergency Unexploded Ordinance Disposal."

"Is that—" He bit his tongue and looked away. "Sorry. None of my business."

"It's okay. I'm surprised it took this long." Duncan gave him a crooked smile. "I like a man with a little self-restraint," he said, leaning close.

"You do?" Ed rasped. Blood heated as hazel eyes captured him. Like that morning when he'd been pinned by Duncan's will and chest.

Duncan tilted his head and neared. Then stopped. Right before their lips met. It was killing Ed in no small way. "I do," he replied, his breath hot and brazen on Ed's flesh.

A flash fire of lust struck, hardening Ed in his duty slacks with a suddenness that stole his ability to say a single word.

"Still want that kiss?" Duncan purred.

"*Yesss.*" Oh, hell, but did he ever. A kiss and skin and a taste and... He pressed into the truck to try to derail the growing problem, finally settling for hiding it when his dick pulsed harder. Dropping his gaze, he fought for control.

He'd never been around anyone who made him feel like this, who could get to him so quickly. Never felt a raging hunger like this. If he'd been attracted to anyone—even Chris—in comparison, what he felt around Duncan made his heart race and his knees shake.

* * * *

Duncan broke down the obstacle course and loaded all the sections into the bed of the truck. Ed volunteered this time, but Duncan wasn't going to argue the help. He wanted to get to the next thing on the night's list.

Which would be getting to know those lips on a very personal level. He closed the tailgate of the truck after a last check that everything was strapped down. "Are you off duty?" he asked Ed.

"Yeah. Not my weekend, but since I'm paid crew I had to be in uniform."

"Nice," Duncan offered. He inched closer, both hidden on the blind side of the truck. He hooked a finger into the waist of Ed's pants. Distance closed until they were nearly touching. "Where?"

Ed gulped. Duncan swore he shivered.

"My place? It's not big but it's private."

"Do you have a bed?"

"Yes."

Duncan pressed a cheek to Ed's. "Then what are you waiting for?"

Ed whined. It was a quiet, breathy sound and it shot straight to Duncan's dick.

"F-follow me?"

Duncan let his breath ease over the skin beneath Ed's ear. "What do you think?" A tease, a promise, Duncan swept his thumb over the telltale ridge in Ed's pants. Muscles clenched. *Gorgeous. Positively gorgeous.* "Go," he ordered gently. "And drive carefully."

Ed took a step away and Duncan allowed him to slip free. "Margo, heel." She zipped to his side and he opened the rear door for her to get into her crate. With her safe and secure, he slid behind the wheel, buckled up and drove around to the street to wait for the yellow Jeep.

It was an uncomplicated drive to Ed's. He thought the house seemed a little too floral for someone like Ed when they pulled up the drive, not discovering the detached garage until he continued around to the rear. This was more Ed. Simple, sturdy. Quiet. Duncan hoped to put that last to the test.

"Is it okay to bring Margo inside?" he asked getting out when he'd parked behind Ed.

"Sure. I don't have any pets, but she'll be okay."

Margo trotted at his side when he joined Ed at the door.

"Come on in," he invited, sweeping the door open. "It's not much but it's home."

"A roof and electricity have a lot to offer," Duncan said. He shut the door behind them, his eyes on Ed. "Margo, go lay down." He pointed to an unobtrusive corner and she went with a sideways glance and a sigh. She'd be asleep in two minutes after the day they'd had.

Duncan was caught by surprise when Ed captured him and backed him with unrelenting strength into the door. A groan sliced through the quiet and then Duncan was being kissed. Hard.

He plowed fingers into Ed's hair and clung, holding him as they battled for control of the kiss. It seemed the shocked arousal Ed had experienced earlier had morphed into something stronger and far more determined. Duncan ate it up.

Solid muscles and a broad chest pinned him and Duncan gripped in answer, wrapping his arms around Ed. A gasp for air and Ed was thrusting, demanding, and conquering. Duncan sucked on that tongue, meeting his attack with one of his own. Duncan *did* promise to kiss him senseless.

"Bedroom," Duncan growled.

Ed moved them off the door and through the compact space of his apartment. Duncan followed his steps like a dancer, never losing those lips. He waited and when Ed's weight shifted, he shoved, toppling Ed to the bed.

Duncan didn't waste a second, stripping the thin belt and loosening Ed's pants before he could get his bearings. "Motherfucker, that is fantastic." He couldn't believe the body this man had. Solid from stem to stern with a dick that was perfect in every sense of the word. And he was about to enjoy every single inch.

"Duncan."

Duncan yanked Ed's clothes open and lowered his head. The smooth skin of Ed's dick was heaven on his tongue. Ed grunted then whined. The broad tip rode deeper, the musky scent driving Duncan to take more. He moaned and his eyes closed, loving the taste.

Ed panted, thrashing from side to side. "Fuck. Too fast!"

He slurped to the end. "Did you want dinner and wine?" Duncan teased, flicking the shiny crown with his tongue.

Ed gasped. "No…don't want…to come yet."

"Don't worry, gorgeous. You're going to be very busy for the next several hours."

Duncan heard the whimper that was definitely beginning to grow on him. This big man, this muscle-bound servant to humanity, was quivering beneath his lips. God, the high was amazing.

He fisted clothing, jerking and tugging until Ed was naked from the waist down. Ed handled the rest, ripping his T-shirt over his head. Duncan slid his hand from a knee, over a thigh to rest on his taut abdomen. "Prime, man. Don't know how you ran free for so long."

"Lucky, I guess." It was a rasped reply. Hands gripped at the edge of the mattress, gathering the blankets in bloodless fists as his frame shook in pleasure.

Duncan closed in on the thick proof of Ed's desires, wrapping his lips then his tongue around the smooth tip. Hearing the catch in Ed's breathing was beyond arousing.

The hair on Ed's leg was soft beneath Duncan's palm where he stroked him. The sounds Ed made when Duncan slipped beneath his balls and cupped them were stuttered and raw. Curious what Ed's reaction would be, Duncan eased as much as he could of the fleshy tip into his relaxed throat, and then swallowed snugly around him.

Ed jerked and shuddered before growling, "Fuck!"

Duncan managed a warped grin. He liked that reaction. A lot. Duncan steadied his breathing. Fingers gripped his hair when he dared to tighten his throat again.

"Duncan," Ed cried, hips straining against his mouth.

Duncan eased up, giving his throat a break. He licked underneath, slurping to pop off the swollen tip.

"Fucking insane."

Duncan smirked. *Yeah, he liked it.* He stood and tapped Ed's knee. "On the bed." Ed opened dazed eyes. Duncan popped the button on his jeans, almost gasping as room alleviated some massive pressure. A thrill rushed him when Ed focused on him as he inched further onto the bed. Brown eyes bore into him, full of need and desire.

Duncan toed out of his sneakers and kicked off his jeans. Slipping the top buttons free on his shirt, he then pulled it over his head.

He knew the second Ed saw the prosthetic—the exact same instant he remembered it. Not that it could be missed; the socket clung right below his elbow and ended at his gloved fingertips. He flexed muscles and the fingers responded. It was a surreal moment. No one outside of his prosthetist and Duncan had seen it like this.

"You just going to stand there?" Ed asked quietly.

Meeting his stare, Duncan dropped his shirt to join the pile on the floor. "I'm not removing it."

"I don't expect you to," Ed said. "I am expecting you to finish what you started." He shook the dick in his hand, then jerked his chin toward the dresser. "Top left drawer."

Duncan tried to smooth out the moment, recapture the hunger he'd been drowning in not two minutes before. He stepped to the dresser and slid out the drawer, fumbling around hunting for the condoms, finding them and a half used pump bottle.

"Come here," Ed coaxed.

Duncan faced the man lying so sinfully expectant for him. He neared the bed and when he was close enough to rest on a knee, Ed brought him down, chest to chest.

"Don't care," Ed breathed. He threaded seeking fingers into Duncan's hair and brought their lips together, a slow kiss that rekindled the desire.

Duncan wedged a leg between Ed's, settling into the V of his body.

"Feels so good." Ed sucked on Duncan's lips, then his tongue. He stroked thumbs over Duncan's nipples, the languorous touch shooting a charge of adrenaline into his body.

Duncan expected a withdrawal, tension, a sign Ed was repulsed by the full truth. Instead, he was more than sure Ed was determined to devour him and make him forget everything else in the room.

Chapter Eight

It had been almost five years since Duncan had last been with someone, when he'd still been in the service and before the accident that cost him his hand. He hadn't been able to deal with the pity the loss of his hand engendered in most to even think about sex, or a relationship. His first prosthetic had been a cable-operated pincer claw, and he'd hated it. He'd been angry and cruel. Anyone within verbal striking distance had unfortunately felt it. He'd lost men in his unit. There were still moments it overwhelmed him, though he'd learned how to control it, or simply beat the rush of adrenaline and fear back. He was one of the lucky few who'd received treatment. It had been an uphill physical and emotional battle returning to civilian life after it had all come crashing down on him.

He had to relearn how to function, doing things one-handed when he'd taken two working hands for granted. He'd learned whether it was flesh and bone, or synthetic, it was normal. It was a means. His hand was a tool. It hadn't been an easy transition by any means, but now years later, he thought he was well-adjusted. As well as a man could be.

And in this exact moment, after so long without this particular pleasure, his body was very willing to reacquaint itself with the throbbing power of another's.

Duncan suckled hard kisses down Ed's jaw to his throat. He arched beneath Duncan's lips, panting and clenching as Duncan learned the man's taste. Easing to the side to rest on a hip, he kneaded the warm skin of a shoulder. Rich brown hair was tempting and he slid up into it, massaging behind Ed's ear with a thumb as he did. Duncan glided his hand away from the fall of Ed's hair, down his body until he reached as far as he could with the stretch of his fingertips, halfway down Ed's thigh. The definition on the man was incredible. Duncan was positive the weights at the station were there for more than decoration.

The bounty of that chest was waiting for him and he homed in on the darker skin of a nipple. A shiver was Duncan's reward. Licks grew into light jawing, Duncan diving into the man's skin and loving the taste. He cruised over the expanse of Ed's chest, taking his time, building the enjoyment for them both as he snuck kisses and tender nips ever lower.

A firm push on his shoulder proved he was getting to Ed. Duncan smiled with a hint of wickedness. He glided down the tanned length at his mercy and poked and teased at Ed's stiff cock with the merest tip of his tongue.

The torturous treatment earned one of those throaty whines. For some reason that one sound drove Duncan insane, firing sparks of lust up his spine. Settling, he slid inches between his lips. Like heated silk, Ed filled his mouth and Duncan was in heaven.

Ed moaned when Duncan laved his full length with the flat of his tongue. Letting him go with a wet, suctioned *pop*, Duncan maneuvered lower, taking in a breath of Ed's essence. Raw musk, sweat, and pure male need. "Open up," he quietly ordered.

Ed gripped the back of a leg and propped it high, exposing the secret place that Duncan wanted to get to know very personally.

The bed bounced hard when Duncan dragged an exploratory nail over the outer perimeter. Not too close, but…close enough.

He upped the stakes by using his teeth on firm flesh. It was like playing with a new toy—and seeing how far he could push the man before him.

"Duncan." The hoarse growl of his name stilled him, wanting to make sure Ed was comfortable with what he was doing. When nothing more followed, he returned to his exploring.

When he'd warned Ed he'd be tied up for hours, it hadn't merely been wishful thinking.

Ed's heartbeat was somewhere between hyper and *holy shit!* Duncan's touch was like a strike of lightning—quick as a pulse, deep as bone, and so utterly stunning, he could barely keep up. Little nips of pain, or sweet hints of heat, or kisses, or…

"God," he ground out, panting, completely at Duncan's mercy. It hadn't been all that long since he and Chris had broken up, about a year if he were pressed to say. Except for feeling lonely and restless, he hadn't thought he'd been overly deprived.

Duncan was making him feel out of control and starved for whatever he wanted to give. Shocks rippled upward as the bite of teeth found their mark, only to swiftly move on to another spot, not giving him a second's time to gather himself before the next pleasurable sting. It was on the border between sharp pain and *oh my God* deliciousness. Goose bumps coated his chest when sensations began to layer over the last.

Warm breath bathed flesh then the wet stroke of a bold tongue propelled Ed, his body hunting for more. He clutched at the blankets beneath him when he found what he hungered for. Deep rumbles of pleasure filled the quiet. Slowly his body loosened, his blood heating with powerful need. He gasped, his eyes shooting wide, unseeing when the width of a finger breached him. Between the thickness starting to fill him and growled vibrations on skin, Ed was at Duncan's mercy.

Duncan mouthed over his sac, rumbled purrs slicing upward. Then he touched the hidden bundle inside Ed and he cried out, almost floating as spots danced in front of his eyes. Duncan's pleased laughter should have pissed him off.

He only wanted him to do it again.

The uncomfortable stretch was minimal with Duncan keeping him strung tight. A few minutes later, all those erotic touches disappeared. He blinked, hunting for Duncan. When their gazes connected, Duncan fell forward gently, finding Ed's lips and kissing him. Ed tunneled fingers into the swaying strands of his hair, holding him close. Duncan sucked a breath when they broke apart, then hefted himself above Ed.

He held a condom packet in his fingers, and wore a grin that Ed could only call daring. "Put it on me."

Ed scooted down the bed a little, ripping into the packet as soon as he was settled. Duncan's jaw clenched when skin connected, a sucked breath proof he was as wired as Ed. Dark eyes burned from within with desire as they watched Ed. With a sense of urgency, want, and a craving that was killing him, Ed eased the condom down Duncan's stiff shaft.

Before he could move again, Duncan gripped his hip and urged him to his stomach. A sense of disappointment was hard to hide, not to mention his reluctance. He wanted to *see* Duncan. Wanted to touch.

"Trust me," Duncan breathed against his ear before he moved between Ed's knees. "We're just starting."

Ed swallowed, grasping at bedding as he settled on his stomach, waiting, slowly dying.

"Could spend hours biting on this." Duncan firmly cupped a butt cheek in his right hand. "Perfectly round and tight as hell."

Ed flexed involuntarily and he swore Duncan growled. He ground his hips into the bed, shuddering with a fresh wash of need. "Duncan." It was a plea.

Then the pressure was there, the known burn, and he mewled. Duncan stilled in an instant until Ed's body rolled, asking for more. Ed's frame tilted, hiking his hips upward and Duncan slid home.

"Fuck," Duncan choked out, hoarse and panting behind Ed. "Going to take all of it."

Ed bit his lip until the ache of the stretch morphed into the bliss of pleasure. Duncan moved, a slow withdraw to return, thrusting deep. Ed couldn't help himself and rolled with the motion. Duncan kissed his back, encouraging him. Soon, his entire focus was vacuumed to the man touching him. It surprised Ed that he was letting the passion rekindle rather than diving into release.

This wasn't some wild afternoon hookup to scratch an itch, which was what he'd been half expecting and would have been perfectly fine with.

He moaned, unable to really keep a constant train of thought going. Duncan ground down and Ed buried his face into the bed. The motion was slow and powerful, tender and erotic. His spine arched when Duncan withdrew, riding that one spot that made him see stars. "*Mmm nnnnphf.*"

The heat of Duncan's chest coated his back, firing shivers of torment up Ed's spine. A strong hand kneaded up and over his shoulder. The thrust of Duncan's body into his was strengthening.

Ed clenched, holding him, wanting more. It felt good…so good.

"That's it. Gorgeous motherfucker. Let me know when you're close." It was a little breathless, grunted. Proof Duncan wasn't as in control as he was trying for.

Ed rolled with him, arching to rise into his thrusts. He hadn't felt like this in so long. He bit his lip then gasped. "Duncan," he choked out. Everything in him was humming with pleasure and need, slowly growing into an uncontrollable boil.

Duncan's body heat vanished and he moved away. "Over."

The one gruff word was all Ed needed. Duncan wasn't the type to fill his ears with cajoling flattery. He hadn't expected it considering the conversations they'd already had.

Ed managed to twist and drop to his back, gazing up into dark hazel eyes that were pinned on him, eating him up without blinking.

Moving over him, Duncan filled him in one steady, sure motion and Ed closed his eyes, drowning in the heat.

The urge to come barreled into him. He gasped, groaning low in his chest as Duncan drove deep and hard.

Ed blinked. Heavy-lidded with desire, he focused and landed right on Duncan's gaze. His lips gently parted as he panted. The rawness of the look, of Duncan's touch, melted Ed. He gripped at his length and Duncan's hips stuttered, picking up speed to shout as he pulsed, filling Ed's channel with indescribable heat.

A couple tugs and Ed lost it, tossing on the pillow beneath his head as he gasped, spinning into the stars in his vision.

"Fucking hell," Duncan gasped, bracing on his good hand over Ed's chest. Stray wisps of hair clung to a damp forehead as they both sucked air. Gently, Ed brushed them aside, pinning the length behind Duncan's ear.

With the rush of passionate hunger fed, Duncan lowered and nibbled lightly on Ed's lips, a sweet kiss. The strength behind the man was undeniable, but the afterglow tenderness blew Ed's mind.

He eased a hand playfully into Duncan's hair, massaging, enjoying the closeness as their world returned to normal. Duncan sighed, pressing into the touch. The single response warmed Ed from the inside out.

A few minutes later, Duncan rose to his feet and removed the rubber, going to the bathroom to dispose of it and wash up. He carried the washcloth from the shower in his hand.

"You are incredible, Ed," he said quietly. He swept the damp patch of fabric over Ed's body and chest.

When he was done, Ed told him, "Toss it in the shower." Duncan did and when he came back, Ed lifted the blankets. "Rest for a while?"

Ed caught the hesitant glance, the sidestep as Duncan tried to backpedal. "Take it off if you'll be more comfortable." He put a hand to Duncan's flesh wrist and when Duncan looked right at him, he said, "I don't care that you have a prostheses. You're not the first I've known, and I know it's more comfortable to take it off." He scrunched the blankets further. "Whichever you want, just come here."

Without saying a word, after several very tense seconds, Duncan turned for the bathroom. Ed heard water gurgling in the basin again, then a few minutes later, Duncan returned carrying the fake hand in his right. He laid it and a fabric sheath on the nightstand. Standing beside the bed, he gazed at Ed, his stare so still, Ed saw himself in its darkness. Ed didn't let the appearance of his shortened arm change one atom in his facial expression.

He raised his hand. "Come here. Want to feel you."

Duncan folded hesitantly onto the bed keeping his one arm close to his chest. Ed curled around him, bringing the blanket over them. "For a bit, then I'm going to hold you to your promise."

"Which promise?"

"Fucking me for hours." He said it perfectly straight, without an ounce of inflection on purpose. He didn't want Duncan to feel pressured, even if he did want to spend more time with the man.

A few seconds later, Duncan snorted, then burrowed into the pillow. Slowly, Ed felt him relax.

He took it for what it was, a show of trust that Duncan was sharing with him. Something likely very few saw or knew about the other man. Duncan was an enigma, tough, a fighter, a secret to many, and one of the kindest, most caring men he'd ever come across.

With a splayed hand resting on the warmth of Duncan's bare hip, Ed closed his eyes, enjoying the shared closeness of body heat and the connection of skin to skin.

Chapter Nine

Duncan sprawled against the wide chest behind him, strong arms binding him close. Featherlight finger strokes tantalized his chest, teases meant to touch and connect, not to arouse. Ed slouched against the headboard, both lazily watching shadows move through the bedroom as the sun went down, each lost in their own thoughts. He needed to head home, but it had been a long time since anyone had held him like this. He was reluctant to break the spell surrounding them.

Few words had been said. There was an easiness that permeated the air. When Ed had awakened from their little catnap, he'd tugged until Duncan rose up on the bed to lean into him. Now they sat, chest to spine, easy and in no hurry for anything else. The occasional brush of lips slipped by his temple.

It was comfortable.

"I want to see you again, just so you understand that," Ed said. The quiet rumble of his voice vibrated skin to skin.

Duncan didn't reply right away. That wasn't to say he hadn't enjoyed being with Ed. He had. He nuzzled against the hard male wall behind him to let him know he'd heard. Duncan hadn't really thought about more than today. He'd lucked into an afternoon with Ed. He hadn't come into this expecting more.

"You know I live more than two hours away, right?"

"So? I work crappy shifts." A strong hand broadened, flattening over Duncan's chest. "What do you do?"

"Insurance reports from home."

"Why don't you teach? You're amazing and Margo is unbelievable."

"I don't have the patience for it," Duncan answered truthfully.

"Then how'd you train Margo?"

Duncan smirked, hearing the wraparound logic Ed was trying for. "I trained with her for a lot of it. I don't have the patience to teach another person. Animals? Maybe. People? Fat chance in Hell."

Ed's chest rocked with a guffaw. "At least you're honest."

"You asked."

Ed laughed roughly. "I bet you get a shitload of compliments on your hair." Fingers threaded through the strands to let them fall. The casual caress relaxed him.

"Not really. I don't talk to a lot of people face to face. Mostly emails."

"So, am I going to get to see you again?"

Duncan had expected another inane type of comment. He let out a breath. "Ed. I don't do relationships."

"Wasn't asking for one," he returned unfazed. "Didn't think spending time, hanging out, being friends, constituted a relationship, well, other than the friends part." Ed's arms cinched around Duncan's middle and heaved him up higher on Ed's chest.

Duncan grunted then settled. "Damn. Gonna just throw me around?"

"Maybe over my shoulder," Ed teased. "I am a fireman." He bit at Duncan's shoulder. "Solid, but I bet I could take ya."

Duncan groaned, half at the playful jest and half at the shot of pain turning into erotic heat on his shoulder. He gripped at the arm pinning him to the wall of muscle at his back. Duncan liked rough, and if a few bruises showed up, he was okay with that. The only thing he wouldn't put up with was rough only to cause pain. He liked physical. He liked force. He didn't stand for abuse. He'd seen all the pain and agony one man could stomach, and then had a full helping for dessert.

He also accepted his personal tastes and desires weren't exactly normal. At least, not that he'd found.

His groan rumbled thickly as Ed raked teeth from where he'd been snacking on Duncan's shoulder up his neck. Blood pulsed and his toes curled. Duncan lolled on his neck and the invitation was clear enough. Ed clamped down like he wanted to audition for a vampire cameo.

"Shit," Duncan growled. He ground his hips into the hard frame holding him captive. Unrelenting arms locked him in place. Ed slid a hand down Duncan's abdomen and teased the flesh of his groin. Teasing had definitely taken a turn toward arousing. And Ed wasn't being hesitant in making that clear when he gripped Duncan's thickening cock.

Duncan swept a hand up, reaching for hair and finding it. "Fuck, yeah. Harder." He moaned hoarsely when Ed followed directions. Then the hand wrapped around his dick began to move. He raised his hips, driving into that constricting band of fingers and hissed as pleasure lit up his senses.

"Stay. Still," Ed said with direct intent, then hooked a foot over a leg to enforce it.

Duncan's heart pounded. Held immobile, clinging to Ed's hair, his other arm pinned beneath the one wrapped around his middle, Duncan was at Ed's mercy as he stroked his dick and raked him with teeth and tongue.

The prison of Ed's hand was fierce, clutching to the edge of pain. Shivers chilled Duncan with each flex as blood coursed and pulsed with a raging beat through veins right beneath skin.

He panted, his chest jumping with each staggered gasp.

Glancing down, the tip of his cock was swollen and shiny with precum, a bright plum ready to be picked.

Ed released him to dig deeper, finding the aching sac of flesh beneath. Duncan's spine snapped ramrod straight when he grasped them, holding the pair then twisting and tugging on each nut until he thought he'd scream. Ed rolled them upward in his palm, shaping them into the shaft of his engorged dick, molding them like clay as Ed wrapped them up and around.

"Will you let me fuck you?"

Duncan shuddered. "I don't..." He shook his head as sensation sliced his frame in two. Ed was a master of torture with four fingers. "Never," he gasped, realizing he hadn't given a full answer.

"No one, ever?" Ed bit down on his pulse point and gnawed with raw strength.

Duncan clawed at the hair in his grip, needing to feel more, burning from the intensity.

"I don't get fucked," he finally managed.

Ed huffed in frustration. "You and Chris. Figures," he grumbled.

Duncan wasn't sure if he was expected to say anything to that, but any words lodged in his throat when Ed wrapped his cock again and pumped him with a slow tug, pinching right beneath the crown.

Duncan's head thumped into Ed's shoulder, his body striving for more, only to be caged beneath a very strong leg and an unrelenting arm.

"Forget it. I get this if I can't have your ass."

"Fuck," he gasped. Duncan would have gone limp if he hadn't been stretched tight as a high-wire.

Ed couldn't hide his disappointment. How did he keep finding these guys who couldn't share? He had no problem being on bottom, but…Christ, give a man a break. He loved to feel the heat when he's slamming home, loved the way a man's body would give beneath him, bowing to him both physically and sexually. Chris wouldn't allow it. Ed hadn't fought hard then, but after their breakup he'd vowed the next guy wouldn't be so unbending. He wanted someone who wanted him as much, who could enjoy the sex as much as he did.

Maybe it was just as well Duncan didn't want a relationship. Ed didn't want to get knee-deep only to have to concede simply to be with someone. So for tonight, he was going to please the shit out of Duncan, make him burn with need and desire. Then they'd go their separate ways with the memories.

Duncan was keeping his one arm close, though it was easily pinned to his chest beneath Ed's own forearm. His other was knuckle deep in Ed's hair, clutching as if he was in freefall.

Ed swept his thumb over the slit at the top of Duncan's dick, spreading the pearl liquid. Duncan's shoulders rocked with excitement. Ed wasn't taking it easy on him, yet Duncan was eating it up. He stroked the engorged shaft in his hand, and Duncan kicked out a leg, opening himself for more.

Scooping up heavy balls, Ed ground them against the hard thickness, rolling everything under his palm, massaging with controlled strength.

"Shit," Duncan hissed. "Not going to last if you keep that up."

"That's the point," Ed informed him. "This one is my call."

Duncan's entire body shuddered. Ed may not get all of what he wanted, but he did know how to make Duncan feel good. He could push buttons, dare to walk the edge a little, especially if Duncan seemed to be turned on by strength and power.

He added a twist to his upward motion, right at the tip and Duncan cried out, quieting to a needy, growled whine that didn't sound like Duncan at all, which made it even sexier.

"Going to make you come so hard," Ed told him.

He shifted a little, swiping fingers over Duncan's chest, to rake and pinch at taut skin, then gradually increased speed and pressure on Duncan's dick. Muscles trembled up and down Duncan's splayed frame as he surged and fought to do something to hurry Ed along but there was nothing he could do—it was all Ed's game.

The fingers tunneled in his hair fell away to grip at the bed, at Ed's thigh, anything to give him leverage. Ed was big enough and strong enough to keep him right where he wanted him.

Liquid streamed from Duncan's cock and Ed used it to slick skin. He could feel every beat of Duncan's heart, every flex of muscle, as he tried to take control and reach orgasm.

When he was sure Duncan was about to scream and beg, he changed everything. He disentangled himself and slid from behind Duncan, letting him collapse to the bed heaving for air. Ed twisted and engulfed his length in one swallow, sucking like he'd be the last of Ed's life.

"Aaaaahhhh! Fuuuuck!"

The shout filled the room right before the first blasts filled Ed's mouth. He didn't stop until Duncan lay before him, a hollow husk of panting man. Breathing heavily, with blood pulsing and raging with the need to come, Ed straightened, gazing down at the stud on his bed. Spitting on his hand, he clutched his own dick and pumped, grunting as shocks sliced upward. Skin tightened and he gasped, then he let the rush of release sweep over him, pulsating fireballs that erupted from within to shoot his seed over Duncan's lower body in stripes and drips.

He sagged onto his knees and then fell to a shoulder beside Duncan on the bed, drifting in a shared state of euphoria as they both caught their breaths.

No, he didn't get to fuck him, and that was okay. Duncan was a good guy. That was in and of itself a remarkable truth. They had a great afternoon together, a good day spent, ending with fabulous sex.

Ed wouldn't build more into this afternoon than what it was. At least now he knew without a doubt he wasn't going to settle. He wanted it all. Not a half relationship, not a guy who would only accept one rule, offer only half of what Ed needed.

In that, Duncan had done him a favor. He would miss the other guy, and maybe they could stay friends, but if Duncan refused to give Ed what he needed... Then he'd have to keep looking. There was someone out there for him.

Chapter Ten

Labor Day faded. September rolled into October. Duncan still took Margo to the park. The leaves were starting to change, faint but there. A sign of the seasons, and of the hot and dryer than normal year, he supposed. He shared a hello but not much else with the brunette jogger. He guessed she'd taken the hint when he didn't encourage conversation, or enough interest to interrupt her run.

He threw the Frisbee for Margo and she raced after it, launching with a grace that never failed to astound him. Trotting back to him, her tail wagged like a machete slicing the air. He knelt in front of her, roughing her a bit with a hand at her neck. She slurped him with a long tongue. They'd already been at the park most of the morning. Duncan was caught up and bored.

After gathering his backpack and attaching Margo's leash, he loaded her into her crate in the truck and drove home. Going through the rituals of water for both, then cleaning up and storing things, he was done and wandering aimlessly within half an hour.

His roving gaze landed on his phone. He could call Ed. Duncan had never given a firm yes or no on seeing the other man again and for some reason, when he'd left Silo, Ed hadn't demanded one. He could have sworn Ed had been interested. Maybe he'd misread him.

They'd lazed in bed for about an hour after they'd cleaned up before Duncan dressed and came home for the night. That had been an incredibly busy day. There had been so much going on for the fundraiser at the station, then later at Ed's. He'd made it home, put Margo to bed and promptly passed out for almost ten hours. Duncan hadn't called, but then neither had Ed. He hadn't been back to Silo either.

Pulling out his wallet, he dug for the slip of paper that had Ed's number on it. Should he call? Holding the paper scrap, he debated. Did he want to see Ed? Actually, he did. He wasn't sure what they'd do, but maybe they'd agree on something.

If that something was sex, well, he wasn't going to complain.

Palming the phone, he dialed the number. It surprised him when he got an answering machine and his shoulders slumped a bit.

"Hey, Ed. It's Duncan. I guess you're on shift. Call when you get this." He left his number in case Ed had lost it or something. Hanging up, disappointment sank in hard. He hadn't considered what he'd do if Ed hadn't been there, or if he'd be on shift duty.

Sighing, he dragged himself over to sit in front of his computer and see if there was anything to keep him occupied.

A few hours later, his phone rang. Contemplating dinner in the kitchen, he reached for the phone and notched it between his shoulder and ear to be able to stare unhindered into the abyss of the refrigerator. "Hello?"

"Hey, Duncan. You called?"

"Yeah, wanted to see when you were off," he said. Maybe they'd catch a movie, dinner, something. Cabin fever was closing in, and there was no cure in sight.

"Not until tomorrow, but I have to go to Stiller Springs. Need to see my mom and dad."

"Oh, okay." He closed the refrigerator door, even more bummed.

There was a moment of silence then, "You want to come? We could get something to eat."

"I don't want to interfere with your time with your folks."

"Dad won't mind meeting you. Mom might, but she won't remember. Early stage Alzheimer's."

"Sorry to hear that," he replied.

Ed made a low sound, a commiseration of sorts. "It's why I need to go. Haven't been in a couple of weeks, and Dad wants me to talk to Mom. She may be declining."

"Wow," Duncan breathed. He leaned on a shoulder against the fridge corner. "Are you sure you want me to come?"

"Actually, the more I think about it, I think I do. If you don't mind being used for a getaway excuse."

Duncan coughed a laugh. "I don't mind. Will Margo be okay, or do I need to find a sitter?"

"Nah. Bring her. She's a good kid."

Duncan grinned. "Okay, what time?"

They firmed up details and by the time Duncan hung up, he was feeling pretty good about making that phone call.

The next day, Duncan's pack lay on the front seat with Margo tucked into her crate for the drive. They arrived at Ed's about midmorning and after Margo had a quick romp and break, they all piled into Duncan's truck for the drive to Stiller Springs.

"Are your folks retired?" Duncan asked.

"Mom is. She was a school teacher for thirty-five years."

"Wow. Your dad?" Duncan tossed a peek at Ed.

"He works for one of the local fisheries. Habitat and breeding."

"That's different."

"He has degrees, just don't ask me about them. I get lost."

Duncan chuckled warmly. "They sound like a nice pair."

"I can't complain. They do their best. Mom took off a couple of years when she had me, but being a teacher was in her blood. Gramma was a teacher too, in Ohio." He twisted a hair on the seat to gaze toward Duncan. "What about you?"

Duncan shrugged. "Not much to tell. I was fostered a time or two, then went into the military when I graduated hoping to make a career out of it."

"You were an orphan?"

Duncan usually didn't like talking about it, but he'd started the conversation. It had been meant to break the silence, not that he'd really intended to divulge dirty secrets. He tipped his head, putting his thoughts in order. He did this to himself. "Yeah. I was apparently abandoned at a hospital."

Ed's shocked silence said everything. There weren't words to convey the reality of such a beginning.

"All they had was my name, day of birth and city, no parentage. I was three."

"Why weren't you adopted?"

Duncan glanced across the truck. "They spent two years trying to find parents or relatives and by then I was starting school. I wasn't exactly a nice kid."

"Oh?" Ed asked with drawled curiosity.

"I was a disciplinary action waiting to happen." He drew a deep breath, his one hand flexing over the steering wheel. "I acted out a lot when I got older. Never physically hurt anyone, or anything, but I was angry. Very angry."

"So you went into the military to channel some of that?"

"It was the military or jail."

"Wow. It's hard to imagine you as a bad boy."

That made Duncan laugh drily. He wondered what Ed would think if he'd seen him back then on his motorcycle. His hair was long now. It was much longer then. "Good. It's been a long time since I let that part of me go."

"You don't even have any tattoos. And you're so good with Margo."

Duncan flicked a glance from the mirror to the crate unconsciously. "Never wanted one. As for her, when I was discharged, I wasn't staying very focused. Rage was trying to reform and I needed something to direct my energy into. Rehab wasn't enough. She actually saved me as much as I did her from the shelter." The overflow of raw emotion had compounded his PTSD symptoms, which had made his rehab especially difficult.

"You can see it," Ed offered thoughtfully. "She's so eager to make you happy." A moment passed. "That does explain a little more though. I don't guess we ever had a chance either." Ed turned to look the other way out the window. "Sucks hard donkey balls, Duncan."

"Why?"

"Not important." Ed sighed and fell silent.

Duncan didn't push, but he was pretty sure he knew why Ed was frustrated. He wasn't good at those kinds of concessions. Relationships. Fucking for fun he had down pat.

Though he was actually a little sorry he was hurting Ed, disappointing him. He didn't like that his rejection was disturbing him, which was in turn bothering Duncan. He'd never really thought about or cared about anyone he'd been the slightest friends with, and if there had been a lover, he couldn't bring a face to mind. There had been few enough faces he'd seen twice as it was in his history.

Ed didn't offer much more than directions, leaving both to mull over their thoughts, as they drove through Stiller Springs. Winding through a subdivision, Duncan spotted neat lawns and colorful decorative pottery with flowering plants draping in freeform from them. Several houses had rose bushes and quaint walled-in flower beds. In his mind, only a retiree would have the time for the upkeep. The time needed for that was partially behind his decision to rent the duplex. All that yard crap was handled by the landlord.

"That one." Ed pointed to a silver Honda sitting in a driveway. Duncan stopped at the curb.

"Did you grow up here?"

"Dad bought it when I was in the seventh grade, so sort of." He unlatched the belt and swung open the door, standing and stretching on the curb at the edge of the yard.

Duncan let Margo out after clipping her leash to her collar, then quietly trailed Ed to the front door.

Ed rang the doorbell and waited.

Duncan wanted to say something, but didn't know where to start. He knew what Ed was looking for. He'd made it clear during Duncan's visit for the fundraiser. He simply didn't know how to bring it up again. Not to mention the really bad timing.

"Hey, Pop," Ed greeted the older man when he opened the door.

"Good to see you." A stray look went over Ed's shoulder to Duncan. "Is this the fellow you talked about?"

Ed inched to the side. "Duncan and Margo."

"That's nice." His dad eyeballed both, including a lingering study of Margo before he widened the door. "Come on in."

"How's Mom?" Ed asked once they were inside.

"Not so good. In the kitchen, writing up a grocery list."

"Oh?" Confusion was clear in Ed's tilted head.

"She went yesterday and doesn't remember." His dad looked tired, and more than a little concerned, though he tried to hide it as he turned his attention to Duncan.

Duncan noted Ed's frown before he could turn away. When the door was shut behind them, he curled the leash around his wrist and held out a hand. "Nice to meet you."

"You too. Go ahead and sit." He faced his son. "I'll let your mother know you're here." He turned to leave them.

Ed said, "Might as well get comfortable. This isn't looking too good."

"Is this worse than before?"

The sorrow in Ed's eyes answered him.

Duncan chose a seat. "Margo, down," he commanded gently. She stretched out at his feet, watching.

Chapter Eleven

Ed moved around the living room, looking for differences, hunting for anything that would give a bigger clue to his mother's state of mind. Everything appeared to be the same as it had been for years, even down to the blown glass roses his father had bought as a gift for one of their wedding anniversaries. Seeing how worried his dad was, Ed now wished he'd made this trip alone. It wasn't right to make Duncan sit through this. He waited with his hands in his jeans pockets, his stomach binding into a knot with all the worst-case scenarios he could envision running through his mind.

"Edward."

His mother's call pulled him around from viewing the room. "Hi, Mom." He gave her a kiss when she gathered him for a hug. He'd outdistanced her height before he was fifteen, so she felt small and delicate in his arms now. "Came into town to run errands and thought I'd see how you and Dad were doing."

"Oh, fine. Fine." Her hands bounced in a wobbly flutter. "Who is your friend?"

Duncan had stood when she entered the room and he offered a hand.

"This is Duncan. Remember? I told you about him and his dog doing the searches." Though he had his doubts she did remember. Her expression was serene, giving away very little.

"Right." She smiled for Duncan. "Nice to meet you."

"You, too."

"Let me get you some tea."

"That's okay, Mom. We can't stay too long."

Her eyes widened with surprise. "Why not?"

"We need to be someplace soon with Margo." He hated to lie, sending a telling glance toward Duncan in his seat again, but he didn't want to be trapped either. At least now they could leave when they were ready.

"We who?"

Ed stuttered to a stop and gazed at the guileless curiosity on his mother's face. He looked toward his father and he shook his head. Sadness darkened his dad's features. Ed's first assumption was correct. Her recent memory was lapsing.

"Duncan and I," he answered gently.

Blank brown eyes swept over Duncan in the chair. "Okay."

He released a quiet breath when it looked like the tangent had been clarified enough for her. He didn't want to upset her. He sat on the couch next to Duncan's chair, leaning forward at the edge.

"So, tell me what you've been up to," he cajoled. "Any late night parties with the church ladies?"

She sat in a chair nearby. "Oh, no. Just the usual card game after Sunday lunch."

Ed hid his wince but didn't refute her. She hadn't played cards in fifteen years. "Is Mrs. Elders still the champ?" Another testing question.

"Oh, no, Edward. Remember? She passed away. She was such a good hostess though."

Ed nodded, filing that away. "Lose anything lately? Dad said you had a heck of a time with your keys last week."

"Oh! Yes. I did. And would you believe they were in the kitchen the whole time? Went all over this house twice. I swear he moved them, but he says he didn't." She finished the last on a bit of a whisper.

He laughed quietly at her perturbed state. "It happens. I'm sure he didn't move them. He has his own to lose." He teased his mother, seeing her smile in agreement. He asked her a couple more questions, poking to get a better idea of her mental state, and wasn't surprised by her answers. Hoped for better, but wasn't surprised.

"Tell me a little bit about what you do," she said to Duncan. "Searches, right?"

Ed listened as Duncan gave an abbreviated version of the same spiel he'd given the day of the Labor Day fundraiser at the station. It really amazed Ed how much Duncan knew about the process and how he constantly included and praised Margo. She ate it up, panting and wagging her tail with contented patience.

"She seems like a really sweet animal," his mother pointed out.

Duncan lowered his right hand to scratch behind her ears. "She's my girl."

Ed smiled at the rarely seen tenderness Duncan was letting slip through. Watching him, he was nearly—*nearly*—jealous of a dog.

Not too much later the phone rang.

"Judy, it's for you."

Ed stood and tipped his head to Duncan. He wasn't too proud to use the phone call as an escape hatch. "I'll stop by next week for longer, Mom."

"Okay, honey." They shared a quick hug and he let her go to answer the phone.

"Dad! I'll call in a day or two."

His dad appeared in the doorway between rooms. "Let me walk out with you. Need to get the mail anyway."

Once all three were on the other side of the closed door, Ed sighed. "She's not hurting anything, is she, Dad?"

"No. She's forgetting more, and like the card game, thinking things that happened years ago, just passed."

They strolled unhurriedly up to Duncan's truck.

"Is she going to the doctor yet?"

"She has a second appointment in two weeks."

Ed leaned against Duncan's vehicle while he caged Margo on the other side. "And you're still keeping track of what and when she thinks she is?"

"Yeah." His dad gave him a serious frown. "You think she's getting worse too, don't you?"

"I think so." He raked a hand into his hair, tugging it into wild clumps. "I don't think she's dire yet, though." He was concerned with how fast her memory was deteriorating, and at what level she was forgetting and remembering, but that could be his imagination since he didn't talk to her daily. Maybe the doctor would have a more optimistic outlook.

Tension seeped from his father's frame, replaced by a heart deep grief. "She's a good woman."

"I know, Dad." Ed clasped a shoulder and gave it a squeeze. The strain and worry was showing more in his father's posture. Mom being ill wasn't going to be good for either of them. He swallowed down the lump that gurgled upward on that last thought.

Brown eyes exactly like his rose. "So are you two dating?"

Ed blinked, straightening against the metal behind him. "No. Just friends." He didn't look toward Duncan. He hoped his dad hadn't embarrassed the guy.

With a glance of confusion, it seemed his dad had expected a different answer. "Well, I'll let you two go. Nice to meet you, Duncan."

"You too, sir."

Ed opened the truck and slid in, giving his dad a last look and he hoped, an unworried smile.

"Nice folks," Duncan offered as they drove away.

"Sorry about that."

"Nothing to apologize for. I think I confused your mother. She kept staring at Margo."

Ed understood. She'd asked questions, but there seemed to be lapses in her understanding. He wished he knew what it all meant. "I didn't mean to make it uncomfortable." Especially his dad. He stared out at nothing through the glass.

"So he thought we were dating. It's not exactly insulting."

Ed swiveled enough to study Duncan. "Yeah?"

"Course not. A guy would be lucky to have you."

Any guy but you, right? Ed didn't know why he was pining for Duncan. He'd made it clear that he couldn't be what Ed needed.

What sucked was he was still attracted to him. Knowing what he did hadn't changed that.

Ed did his best to push the lingering and unavoidable thoughts away. "So what else did you want to do?"

"If it's okay with you, I need to run by the pet store I looked up and spoil the pooch, then…" Duncan slid Ed an easy smile. "How about lunch?"

"Sure." He relaxed into the seat. "Thanks for coming, by the way."

"Anytime, man. At least they're cool with you being gay."

"They've had a while to get used to it," Ed explained. "I told them in high school, and no, I couldn't change it." He didn't add that he really hadn't brought many friends, or otherwise, to meet his parents. It had been a gradual curve, but at least they'd been as understanding as they knew how. Ed studied Duncan's profile. "I guess there really wasn't anyone for you to hide from, was there?"

"More than you can imagine. Don't Ask, Don't Tell was in full swing when I was enlisted. Before that? School? Didn't really matter. If anyone wanted to fight, they had one. Being gay was the least of my worries."

"Have you had any boyfriends?"

"Serious ones?" Duncan flipped his blinker and turned onto another street. "No."

"More of that bad boy image, huh?"

Duncan shrugged, bobbing his eyebrows. "Let's say I wasn't hurting for company when I wanted it."

Ed didn't doubt it. The man was undeniably gorgeous. Trim and sleek with muscle and attitude, hair to his shoulders and killer eyes. And he undoubtedly also had attachment and commitment issues. Not that Ed could blame him for those. Duncan had started life with the worst case of abandonment any child could ever suffer. If he went through life with no one at his back, then he had no other foundation to work from. Ed didn't blame him for any walls he'd built because of that, he'd just have to keep himself from wanting what he couldn't have.

They rolled to a stop in front of the store and both got out. With Margo on her leash, they went inside the near warehouse sized store.

"Wow," Ed said. "What don't they sell?"

"The actual pets. Adoptions only. Unless you count the fish."

"Nice," Ed remarked. He trailed Duncan and Margo, who seemed to know exactly where they were, her nose up in the air and her tail going nuts as she poked and sniffed.

Ed's attention was drawn to an aisle loaded with all kinds of chew toys, pull toys, and things that squeaked when squeezed.

He squished a large plush something that made an awful howl of demented squeakiness. He tossed it back on the shelf with a grunt. "That must drive an animal insane," he muttered.

"They all sound like that, or something close to it," Duncan said at Ed's shoulder, picking up another and repeating Ed's squeak of doom. Margo tipped her head and perked her ears in curiosity. "See? They like it." He hitched a shoulder. "I need a new Frisbee and food for her."

Duncan pitched the toy high in the air and Ed caught it with a flip of hands as Duncan chuckled, walking away.

"Ass," Ed called under his breath.

"Uh, yup," Duncan agreed, laughing more.

Putting the toy back, he followed Duncan and his laughter through the store. It wasn't a bad place to be in fact, watching that swagger walk up and down aisles. Duncan stopped and filched a Frisbee out of a pile.

"What do you think?" He held it in front of Margo who wiggled like she was her own earthquake. "Okay." He tucked it under an arm to protect it, grabbing a second to go with it.

"Really likes those, huh?"

"Loves them."

Ed held a twisted rope in his hand, popping it playfully into his palm. "Does she like these?" Looking up he caught Duncan's gaze and grinned evilly. Ed lowered his voice, teasing Duncan at his side by wiggling the rope toy. "Doesn't get exactly stiff, does it?"

Duncan hooted roughly. "I know something that does." He peeked at Ed from beneath lashes, his eyes darkening with a lusting heat.

Duncan closed the gap to stand in front of Ed. His hand drifted to glance against the front of Ed's clothes, hidden by their closeness. Ed sucked a breath. "I like the way this one does," Duncan purred. "Can I play tug with your rope?"

Ed's breathing increased. He wanted to say yes so badly.

Duncan dipped and found Ed's bottom lip with his teeth, a slight bite. A sting. Ed shook. The small tease made blood surge into parts that were better left undisturbed when out in public.

"You're so fucking hot when you get turned on," Duncan growled before straightening in front of him.

"Finding everything okay, gentlemen?" an employee called unseen from the end of the aisle behind Ed.

"Doing fine," Duncan replied without breaking his gaze from Ed's. A few timeless seconds passed before he said, "Could eat you alive."

Ed guessed the employee had moved on. Duncan inched away, and Ed hauled in a sharp and needed breath.

"Ready to go eat?"

"Lunch or…" Ed tried to think about food. Tried to think about dogs and toys, to will his body into behaving. It wasn't listening.

"Right now? Lunch. We'll take care of the *or* very soon."

Ed saw the promise in Duncan's hungry eyes and swallowed the whimper. Ed knew Duncan was only looking for sex, and maybe friendship.

Watching him walk away, Ed decided maybe sex one last time wasn't really giving in. Not if it was only once more, right?

Chapter Twelve

Duncan and Ed slid from the truck in front of his detached apartment. "I'm going to let her run a few minutes."

"Sure. Come on in when you're done." Ed unlocked the front door and vanished inside.

They'd shared an unhurried lunch and relaxed on the ride back. All in all, it had been a nice day. To give Margo a good stretch, he grabbed one of the Frisbees he'd bought and began playing with her. He heard a phone ring and looked over his shoulder. A moment later, Ed opened the door and walked out to him with the phone in hand.

"Got plans for tonight?"

Duncan shook his head.

"Can you stay? Chris is cooking out and asked us over."

Us? "Sure. When?"

Ed spoke into the phone. "Couple hours," he conveyed.

"Okay. I'll have her," Duncan said, inferring Margo.

"She's not a problem at all," Ed replied, turning and going inside, agreeing and confirming.

After a few more tosses, Margo was slowing down and he was ready for a drink. Dropping the toy back into the truck, he locked it and trailed Ed through the door. Ed held out a bottle of water.

"Come here, Margo," Ed called, nudging a large bowl of water for her. She trotted over and slurped herself into doggy heaven.

"Thanks." Duncan held up the bottle, including Margo's with a nod of his head.

"Welcome." Ed slid a finger into a belt loop and tugged Duncan closer. "You sure you're okay with tonight? I told them no, but Jamie said I was nucking futs and to come over anyway."

Duncan's lips twitched. "Jamie said that, huh?"

"Yeah, he's worse than a kid brother."

Duncan drew a slow swallow of water. He licked at his lips, watching Ed do the same. "So, were you and Chris dating?" he asked, waiting for Margo to finish to tell her to go to the corner and sleep.

"For a while, yeah. We broke up before he met Jamie. I tried to take him out, but I think I made Jamie nervous early on."

"Oh?"

"Yeah. He came from a rough household. His dad was an absolute prick."

Duncan shook his head. That sweet guy had been someone's whipping boy? He hated the thought. It was one of the few reasons he was glad he'd never been placed with a family. Fostering had been bad enough. There's little doubt he would have ended up in jail if some fucker had been abusive to him. It's where he'd almost landed more than once *without* being abused.

"A couple hours, huh?" Duncan teased, quickly switching mental gears by rocking his hips against Ed's hand hooked into the belt loops at his waist. "What are we going to do?"

"I thought maybe grocery shopping, or I need to scrub the bathroom, or…"

Duncan chuckled. "Not even close."

Ed's eyes began to glimmer knowingly. "Oh?"

"Oh, yeah." Duncan inched closer.

"Good, because I really hate cleaning the bathroom."

Duncan burst out with a sharp laugh right when Ed roped him physically against his chest with a crooked arm. A slight spin had him pressed into the closest flat space, caged by all that hard strength.

There was no hesitation in Ed's kiss. Duncan grasped him tighter, savoring the heat of chest grinding into him.

A plowed hand gripped at Duncan's hair. He gasped as pleasure burned through his frame. Ed rolled his pelvis and Duncan's jeans immediately grew too small. "Fuck," he groaned.

"Want you," Ed murmured, biting at the soft skin of Duncan's shoulder through his shirt.

He worried the flesh between his teeth, making Duncan's knees weak. Sharp tingles iced his spine as nerves sparked. With one of Ed's hands still immobilizing him by his hair, the other dug beneath Duncan's shirt, rubbing and scratching fleetingly enough to be felt. The button of his jeans popped free with a little help from Ed. Duncan grunted as a fresh wave of blood flooded his already pulsing dick.

Ed was keeping him off balance. He couldn't think. All that muscle… Ed was broader and taller and able to drive Duncan right out of his mind. Dominating a man like Ed was a high he'd never get tired of, except Ed wasn't giving an inch. Duncan shifted, releasing Ed's waist to return the favor, to grasp at him, only Duncan found his wrist captured and his arm braced to the wall next to his head.

"My game," Ed growled.

Duncan panted. "Ed." It was a breathy whine, and Ed was making him do it. The strength was an aphrodisiac. The power behind the control used against him drove him insane. He pushed back and Ed held him.

"You want this, gonna have to earn it," Ed warned over his lips. "I want your ass."

Duncan stilled. "No." Harsh breathing echoed between them. "I can't."

A snarl flared to life for a fraction of a heartbeat. Duncan tensed. He'd never allowed it. Before he could guess Ed's intent, he'd stiff-armed the wrist he'd pinned and crouched, jerking Duncan forward and over a shoulder like a sack of potatoes.

"Fucking shit!" Duncan howled. He jerked, but was held tighter.

"Fucking relax. Not going to rape your ass," Ed warned on a harsh exhale, sounding very insulted. "Don't want to hurt you."

"Could have warned me," he retorted, stiffly unclenching from the surprise move. He couldn't remember *anyone* doing this to him.

"Where's the fun in that?" came the sarcastic reply.

Duncan grunted, now staring upside down at a tautly muscled ass. He goosed a cheek with his good hand.

Ed yelped and hopped, which made Duncan grin. "Payback, asshole."

Ed flipped him onto the bed, then pounced, pinning him as solidly as he had to the door. Duncan's head was spinning from the sudden ups and downs. He groaned when Ed captured his mouth, giving no quarter, dueling and sucking hard on Duncan's tongue. The bed creaked beneath them, the mattress dipping as Ed moved over him. Duncan gripped Ed's side while a hand worked between them to wiggle beneath jeans.

Duncan hissed, his head rearing back when he felt Ed's hand wrap around his stiff cock.

"Want you naked."

Duncan wanted the same thing. He fumbled with his shirt, jerking at buttons until they slid free. Ed worked on loosening Duncan's jeans then dragged them down, tugging them off along with his shoes. Once they were gone, he straddled Duncan and helped him shimmy out of his shirt.

Ed wasted no time in copying him, getting down to skin in seconds.

Duncan ran his hand over Ed's chest, pinching a needy bud between his fingers, enjoying watching Ed toss his head. Rising up on elbows, Duncan homed in on one to suck, laving it with his tongue and finding it over and over between teeth. Ed trembled above him.

"Sexy fucker," Duncan crooned huskily.

Ed sank forward, body to body to kiss him again. "I still want you."

Duncan blinked, shaking his head. "Ed."

"Last time, Duncan," he warned, his voice even. "I like you but I need more."

Duncan swallowed, his mouth opening, but he was silenced unexpectedly by the firm grip of a hand on his genitals. He moaned, his head lolling. *Needed more what?*

He was attracted to Ed. He liked spending time with him. What else did he need? There was no hope of figuring it out with Ed's hands and mouth all over his chest and moving lower. The wicked heat of Ed's tongue lapped Duncan's shaft and balls.

Wet suction over the crown of his dick made his toes curl. Damn, no one gave head like Ed. The man got off on it, hyping the pleasure twofold back to Duncan. He swiveled his hips, and Ed rode the movement. Duncan hissed in pleasure. The intensity was like a flame, rolling and building as Ed engulfed him in tight heat. "Ed," he growled out, feeling the warning sparks start to fly.

Ed let him go with reluctant sips. "Don't move." Ed stood from the edge of the bed and grabbed a condom and lube from the dresser drawer. Duncan hefted onto an elbow, cautiously watching.

"What am I supposed to do if I don't move?"

Ed dropped the condom and lube on the bed. "Do you trust me at all, Duncan?" He frowned.

Duncan eyed what Ed had tossed at his side. "Yes."

"Then relax." He looked down and grunted in exasperation. "Christ. Look at that."

Duncan did and felt bad for killing Ed's thrill. His dick was losing its taut, upright position. He rose a little higher on his propped arm. "Come here." He beckoned with a twitched shoulder.

Ed scooted closer, his neglected dick swinging from side to side.

"I'm sorry," Duncan offered, repentant, cupping Ed's delicious balls in his hand and licking the tip of his softening shaft. Savory and bittersweet, the salty liquid waiting for him on the warm flesh burst on his tongue and he moaned. Lighter fingers than before scooped into his hair, threading into the length to keep him on task. It was the kind of task he enjoyed, mouthing over the head and sucking it into his mouth.

"You look so fucking good doing that," Ed said.

Glancing upward through his lashes, Duncan collided with deep brown eyes, intent on his every action. Another sharp little thrill arced through his frame. He loved having Ed's attention like this. It made his blood race and his heart pound. Proving he was sorry, he spent several minutes repaying the ecstasy Ed had given to him moments before.

Swallowing him deep got a rumbled growl from Ed that made him shiver. He felt Ed bend a little, shifting next to the bed, then found out why. He began to stroke Duncan's cock, sharing the pleasure. Duncan gasped, gnawing, sucking, and licking. He thrust his hips into the fisting action, that slow burn of hunger rising again.

"Lie flat," Ed instructed.

Once Ed rolled down the rubber, Duncan began to get a clue easing his worry. Ed climbed onto the bed and found Duncan's mouth, kissing him hungrily. He palmed Ed's head with his good hand, diving into the demand of the kiss. Blood raced and his skin felt tight, heat surging with each thud of his heart as he lost himself to the desire.

Gasping for air, Ed rose over him and straddled him.

"Hell," Duncan groaned, clenching his jaw. He hadn't done this a whole lot either. If he was calling the shots, it wasn't a position he would naturally choose. A hand on his chest snapped his focus upward and out of his thoughts.

"Not going to hurt you. Just stay still…a minute." Ed was panting by the time he finished speaking. Brown pools rolled up into his head as he sank slowly lower.

Heat encased Duncan in a viselike grip, and both flexed when Ed finally settled, full to the hilt.

"I know you're used to being in control, but not this time."

"Ed." He tried to talk around a dry mouth.

"Trust me," Ed repeated in a whisper, eyes blazing with an unrelenting need. A burning need that was solely for Duncan.

Chapter Thirteen

Ed watched the nervousness and uncertainty flow from Duncan's shoulders. His hands rose and settled on Ed's thighs, petting him lightly. Resting on his knees, he lifted upward and pumped against the thick pole filling him. Ed swore Duncan was hitting every nerve in his body. He didn't know what Duncan's hang-up was, but it had to be huge—he saw it every time they were together in the other man's eyes. Ed didn't think it was him, but it still cut deep that Duncan didn't trust him enough to open up. He knew some never could, but just because Ed also got his thrills by riding didn't mean he didn't like to fuck.

Duncan twitched his hips and Ed's thoughts stuttered. God, he could feel the heavy pulse of his rapid heartbeat through the condom when he touched flesh to flesh. He moaned loudly when Duncan cupped his balls, cradling them as he rose up and down. Enough teasing pressure to make the pleasure last rather than a fireball that would erupt.

Through the fog of it all, he realized he only felt one hand. The left was still resting on his thigh. Not that he didn't want it there, but he wanted all of Duncan's touch and if that meant the leather glove he wore—*Oh, fuck. Leather?*—then he didn't want him to hold back. He didn't want Duncan to think he had to.

"Both hands," he growled thickly.

Startled eyes lifted from the view of where he'd been playing with Ed's nuts.

"Just don't rip anything off." Ed knew he had enough control with it to physically use it.

Duncan's snort was cut short. Ed flexed, making it clear he wasn't done with him. Duncan groaned, his eyes slamming shut. Duncan wasn't half a man, and Ed didn't like the man he was naked with acting like he was.

"I want it," he said, regaining Duncan's gaze.

"But," Duncan said, hesitantly trying to argue.

Ed raised the gloved hand off his thigh and cupped it in his fingers. "It's still you, and I want you to touch me." Proving he knew exactly what he was doing, he rested it over his erection then slid Duncan's right hand from where it teased his groin and brought it to his mouth. "Figure it out. This one is busy." And he began to suck on the digits as he rolled his hips with little jolts, keeping Duncan utterly enthralled and off balance.

Shudders cascaded down Duncan's frame as Ed delivered on his threat, keeping those fingers soundly occupied with his tongue and mouth.

Eyelashes fluttered at the first stroke of leather to flesh, a dry grasp up and down his cock. The leather was a different feel, smooth, cool, but not unpleasant. He wasn't expecting tensile strength, so when the fingers flexed *that* much, he gasped, thrusting into the formed hold. Sparks were building and holy hell, but his balls were feeling it.

"Ed." Duncan's plea was a needy roar underneath the heaves of breath.

"Don't stop, sexy," he encouraged. "Feels great."

Gazing down into those stormy eyes, Ed saw the shocked surprise. With that one look, the raging fire was teetering to explode out of control.

Releasing the hand he was orally adoring, he flexed forward and attacked Duncan's mouth. The drag of the glove retreating made him shiver. *Je-sus.* He couldn't believe how that turned him on.

Then both of Duncan's hands gripped hair, giving leverage to pump fiercely in time with Ed's glides.

"Aw, fuck." Duncan clenched. "Can't stop. *Fuck!*" He shouted with a gusted growl. Choppy and raw, he slammed them together.

Ed couldn't catch his breath. His head arched on his neck as his spine bowed. Friction was building to make him combust. "Yes! Shit! Yes!"

Sound faded and his world shrank. Lava burst through his veins, pulsing like a cannon through his dick to empty onto Duncan's chest. The tight press of their bodies sawed in tandem over his length, milking him through the eruption.

Both of them were desperate for air. Sweat-slick skin slid like oiled silk together. Propped on his forearms, Ed rested against Duncan's shoulder. With a low moan, Duncan's legs stretched flat from where they'd bent up against Ed's flanks. He was still tingling from the power of those legs. Regretfully, when he felt the filling press in his ass begin to fade, he hefted his body free and dropped to Duncan's side.

"Unfucking real," Duncan rasped, sounding utterly fucked out. He raised an arm and dropped it over his eyes. "Fuck, Ed. You killed me."

Ed chuckled, his lungs at least no longer burning. He was still wallowing in the rush himself. "Let's clean up. We still have time before Chris is expecting us."

Duncan limply nodded, still hidden beneath his arm. "You're sure he's cool with me and Margo?" A limp hand stretched and flexed over his sternum.

"Well, he invited Margo. I'm guessing as her transportation, you'd have to come too."

Duncan snickered. "Ass."

Ed grinned and tapped a hip. "Come on." He slid off the bed and grasped an ankle, getting Duncan's lagging attention.

"Okay, okay," he grumped.

Ed led him to the bathroom to gather cloths and a towel.

* * * *

"Nice spread," Duncan said coasting down the driveway about an hour later.

"It was his folk's. His brothers have their own places."

Duncan counted the extra cars already there, and guessed that's who they belonged to.

"They're a handful but all right guys."

"Oh?" He parked the truck beside the last vehicle and got out.

"Yeah, they share the town vet clinic operations together."

"Right. I remember him saying that."

Duncan opened the rear door and let out Margo. She fell in at his side. She always tended to stay a little closer when he was on edge. She'd never been aggressive, but for moral support, she couldn't be beat.

"Bring one of her Frisbees. Tons of room."

"Good idea." Bent over the rear seat, he dug one from the shopping bags, and then jerked straight with a scowl on his brow when a hand cupped his ass cheek. Ed's innocence was so overdone, he laughed. "Perv."

"Appreciating," he corrected, then winked. As they walked to the rear of the house, Ed sniffed and sighed a healthy groan. "Damn, that smells incredible."

Clearing the corner, Duncan spotted a group of guys. He knew Chris and Jamie but blinked when he realized the other two... "Twins?"

"Heh, yeah. Quade and Cade."

Jamie spotted them first. "You brought her!"

"Her?" someone quipped, obviously lost to Jamie's reference.

"This is Duncan and Margo," Ed offered, sharing a handshake with one of the twins. Introductions were made.

It wasn't hard to tell the twins apart between the haircuts and tattoos. "Nice to meet everyone." Duncan shook hands, then nodded to Chris when he waved from the grill.

"Ah, SAR, right? I missed your demonstrations at the fundraiser. Someone had to mind the store," Cade said.

"Quit complaining. It was the slowest Saturday of the year. Everyone was downtown," Jamie pointed out with an impish grin. "He tries so hard for sympathy because that was his weekend."

Duncan smirked but stayed silent. It was pretty clear Jamie could hold his own against the larger brothers.

Jamie motioned to the Frisbee. "Can I?"

"Sure." He handed over the disc.

"Anything I should know?" Jaime asked.

"Yeah, she's insatiable."

Jamie smiled brightly. He lowered and reacquainted himself with Margo. Her tail started to whap the ground as soon as she saw the toy. Jamie called to Margo and after a quick head pat from Duncan, she followed him, bounding really, to play catch.

He happened to catch Ed gazing his way. Deep brown eyes sparkled with life in the sunlight. Something curious shifted inside, a mild flutter hitting his midsection. Guessing it had to do with letting Jamie throw for Margo, he shrugged. "Got a beer?" he asked in general.

"Oh, sure." Cade spun. "Sorry, man. Make yourself at home." He neared a blue cooler and dug a bottle out of ice. "Leaded and unleaded. Jamie doesn't drink a lot." He returned to hand it over adding, "The red one is corn. Don't open it yet."

"Corn?" Duncan popped the top on the bottle and flipped the lid into a nearby bucket where he spotted other bottles and trash.

"Yeah, easier than having a huge pot going. Dump in shucked corn and a couple inches of boiling water, close and steam."

"Cool." Duncan hadn't ever heard of that, but it sounded simple enough. He guessed with six guys, a cooler wasn't a bad idea. "Wow. Expecting more?" He snuck a good look at what filled the grill. Thick and juicy burger patties from edge to edge. He moved nearer, drawn by the sight and oh yeah, that did smell intoxicating: spices, beef, and heat. He licked his lips.

It had been a good long while since he'd had a grilled anything.

Chris smiled broadly and positively without guilt. "Nope. We're not shy about food. Country boys, born and bred."

"Been here your whole life?" Duncan asked, taking a soothing sip of the cold beer.

"For everything except veterinary school. I had a lot of hands-on training with my dad. The boys did a little more school time than I did, for different things. Cade also has a business degree."

"You all work hard, together," Duncan surmised.

"We've fallen into the rhythm, but yeah." Chris tested a couple of patties and flipped a couple of others. "It works for us." He stopped what he was doing and gave Duncan a bottomless stare. "You'd fit in around here, if you ever wanted to."

"Doubt it," he denied quietly.

Chris grew thoughtfully silent for a few minutes. Then, "I've heard people talking about what you did during the tornadoes and after. And about Margo. She has her own fan club at the firehouse. Just ask Ed. Not to mention what you did for us and our neighbors."

Duncan shifted on his feet uncomfortably. "That's gratitude, and it's appreciated, but it's Margo's, not mine."

"No, that's acknowledging what you bring, too." Chris closed the lid on the grill and hung the tongs over the edger bar on the side. "Something to think about if you needed more than one reason."

"More than one reason?" he echoed. His brow furrowed, then he got it. He shook his head as he said, "Ed and I, we're not dating. We're friends. That's it."

Chris gauged Duncan then swept Ed a quick look. "Okay. My mistake. You're still welcome."

Duncan shifted so Ed couldn't see or hopefully hear what was being said. "Why did you think we were?" First Ed's dad that morning, now Chris, and more than likely everyone else there thought he and Ed were... Well, more than they were. What was he not seeing? Because he really didn't want to encourage it.

It made him uneasy, to start.

"Ed's happy," he said simply. "Come inside." He turned on a boot heel and Duncan followed, his stomach tossing now over the wonderful scents of cooked beef and the knot it was trying to become over what Chris was alluding to.

Once in the kitchen, Chris leaned on the counter and crossed his ankles and then his arms over his chest. A thoughtful scowl darkened his features for an elongated moment, then he sighed. "I guess Ed told you we were together before I found Jamie."

Duncan nodded, sipping his beer, keeping silent.

"He's a good man, Duncan. I hurt him, and I'm lucky to still have him as a friend. His life is here. The life he wants to live, is here."

"His parents are only an hour away," Duncan mentioned.

"They are. That makes Silo comfortable for him. Silo is also an inclusive community. Three of our township leaders are gay or lesbian. You want to raise Cain? Piss them off." A small smirk flicked over his mouth then vanished.

Duncan huffed but understood the warning. "So what you're saying is it would be a very hard choice for him to leave, if he wanted to at all."

"Yeah, I am." He straightened and reached into a cabinet for a large platter, closing the door with a soft wooden thud. "I'm not pushing you one way or the other, but if you like Ed, keep that in mind. I still care and want him happy." Chris' gaze grew sharp as he faced toward Duncan. "If you're only playing with him, then do us all a favor and don't come back. He doesn't need that. No one does."

"Ouch," Duncan quipped on a breath.

Chris crossed the kitchen to leave, but paused at Duncan's shoulder. "And if you think for a second your hand means dick to any of us, you're fucked in the head."

"Sure you're not still in love with him?" Duncan jeered. It sure sounded like he harbored some kind of residual emotion for the other man.

"I never was," Chris replied, tinged with sadness. "That was the hardest part between us. I never was."

Duncan touched him with his left hand right as he turned away, but when he tried to speak, the words got lodged in his throat.

Chris' expression didn't exactly soften, but he did seem to understand. "You need to ask him, Duncan. All I can tell you is what I see when he's with you."

With that parting wisdom, Chris left him standing in the kitchen. Following out the rear door a few seconds later, Duncan spotted a stranger talking to Jamie. Cade, Quade, and Ed were watching close by, with Chris a mere few feet apart from the pair talking. Even Margo seemed to be watching with a protective, attentive posture.

An envelope was handed to Jamie and after a final few words, the man turned and slipped into a car to drive away. Jamie stood silently, staring at the car then the envelope in his hand. Distracted, he sluggishly spun and hunted for Chris, walking up to him to immediately be swept into engulfing arms.

"What was he doing here?" Chris growled, glaring out after the car's departure.

"He sold the house." Jamie swallowed heavily. Everyone crowded closer in support to hear. "He's going to stay at a hospice. He has terminal cancer." Jamie shuddered through a shaky breath. "Dad apologized." He tipped on his neck to stare up at Chris. "He actually said he was sorry."

"Are you okay?" Chris swept hair away from Jamie's face.

"Yeah. It's a shock, but so long as he's at peace with what he's doing then I'm okay with that."

Duncan noticed Ed had moved close to his shoulder. "Remember when I told you he came from a bad situation?" he offered quietly. "That was his dad."

Jamie tugged Chris down for a quick kiss, whispering in his ear. With a nod from Chris in answer, Jamie went inside and Chris started unloading the grill.

"He's going to set the table. Grab the coolers. Let's go eat." Chris smiled, slowly relaxing after their unwanted and unexpected guest.

Chapter Fourteen

Ed was reluctant to release the buckle in Duncan's truck that evening. They'd eaten until they couldn't suffer another bite at Chris', then hung out until Cade had to leave to take care of the animals at the clinic for the night. It had been a while since they'd all gotten together like that. Ed missed the closeness. What made it better was having Duncan to share it with, but he knew after tonight...

He finally pushed the safety button. No point in drawing out the next few minutes. "So, I guess this is it," he said. The belt slid away and he stared ahead to the front of his rented garage apartment. He refused to acknowledge the hollowness growing within his chest. He'd known this was going to be the outcome, and he'd allowed himself to want it anyway. It was too bad Duncan hadn't shown any signs of doing anything different.

Even at Chris', there'd been wall, a distance. Ed had hoped there would be *something* there, but it was clearly all in his head and tied up in his own desires. Duncan wasn't going to let him get close.

Ed would be the first to admit he was curious about what Duncan and Chris had vanished to talk about, but if Duncan wasn't sharing, he wasn't begging.

"Ed." Duncan's chin dropped.

Ed heard the regret even if he didn't say the words.

"Don't. I don't want excuses. I get it. You're too proud, dominant, scared, whatever to be *that way*." He popped open the door. At that point, it really was no surprise to him how his heart ached with having to say goodbye this time. "I'm sorry too, Duncan. You were damn close to perfect enough for me."

"Damn it," Duncan snapped a growl. "It's none of that." He stiffly leaned back, sagging his head to the bench headrest behind him. Open eyes stared upward at nothing. "I have PTSD. It's impossible for me."

Ed slowed his exit. "Post-traumatic stress disorder?" He hunted over his shoulder, twisting on the seat to more clearly view Duncan in the fading sunlight.

Duncan closed his eyes and exhaled with control. "I lost more than my hand, Ed," he intoned levelly. He didn't open his eyes. Didn't look toward Ed. "I lost two of the closest guys I'd ever called brothers, the only family I'd ever really had." A shudder rocked his chest. "The damage to my hand couldn't be repaired. I had it all. Shrapnel, burns, and bone damage. That's why they took it." His voice had fallen to monotone, a recital of abstract details.

Ed wondered if he was even aware of the minute flexing of his left hand, a phantom effort to feel what had once been so very real. "And how many did you save?" Ed asked sincerely.

Duncan lolled his head on the seat, his eyes glassy and filled with pain. "Five of my team lived."

"Did you ever think that they were as grateful to you for saving them as you are feeling guilty for not saving the two you couldn't?" Watching him, there was one thing Ed felt down deep. Duncan shouldn't be alone, shouldn't be leaving right that minute.

He reached out, cautiously, but letting Duncan know what he was doing as he stroked his chin. "Come inside." Ed nearly held his breath waiting for the other man to make his choice.

Relenting, Duncan nodded and released his belt. Once he was clearly moving from behind the wheel of the truck, Ed slid out and walked around the front to join him. He didn't want to take a chance until Margo was on the ground with them that Duncan might second-guess himself and try to leave.

With Duncan at his shoulder, Ed unlocked the door and let them both in. Margo patiently waited and at the last minute, Duncan seemed to remember to give her a command to go to a corner. Using light fingers, Ed captured Duncan's hand and tugged him to the couch when Duncan seemed satisfied Margo was going to obey. "Sit." Duncan sank down like every bone in his body was weary. "Tell me." *Help me understand.*

Duncan's entire body shook. His eyes began to glaze over again, staring upward, but Ed was sure he was seeing everything as clearly as he had that day.

"Incendiary weapons are a bitch," Duncan rasped. "The Taliban wasn't shy about using anything within their grasp. Gunpowder, gases, bleach, TNT." He paused, and the tone of his voice changed, grew hollow. "Do you know how much damage a fraction of an amount can do?"

When Ed feared Duncan was going into a dark place inside his own head, he cupped his flesh hand and held on tight. "You're here. Not there. Remember that."

Duncan swallowed. "I'm trying." Time ticked past. "We had orders to trail battle waves and dispose of any little gifts. Leftover shells, mines, homemade and timed bombs could be especially nasty. It had been a very quiet hunt up 'til then that day. We'd searched two buildings and were going into our third when the firefight started. The area was supposed to be secure. They had us flanked on two sides, trying to pin us. That was when I knew we were in trouble." He paused, swallowing thickly.

Ed took advantage of the small break. "You were the squad leader, weren't you?"

"Close enough, but yeah. Those were my guys." He clutched his hand into a fist, gripping Ed's hard. "That was when the rockets hit. We had to get out of there. Find a better place to hole up for the guys on the ground to get to us."

Ed didn't complain when the hold on his hand increased to a near crushing pain. Duncan wasn't in the room with him. That was clear.

"When everything went to shit, I remember telling them to help Brokaw and Jacoby. I didn't know they'd sustained fatal shrapnel wounds from the explosions. Fuck, all I knew was we had to get out of there. And then the big one came. I shoved the closest and ordered...something. It took me out instead of my entire team. That was the last real thought I had, trying to move to a better location for cover."

"You made sure they were safe, Duncan," Ed said.

Slowly, the tension rippling across his upper frame eased. Dark lashes fluttered. "The rest of it, from what I was told, was fought and done in less than five minutes. It was a small scout group that had snuck in overnight. They had our number that day."

Ed had never seen anything like what Duncan had lived through. Even large structure fires were usually infrequent, and he doubted a person in town could remember the last explosion one had caused.

"You have to realize, you did what you could."

"Some days I do. Others…" He shrugged. "Every now and then, something triggers an episode, a nightmare, or a memory. I definitely hate loud explosions. I have a drawer full of earplugs." The grip imprisoning Ed's hand lessened, followed by a single squeeze to simply stay in contact. Duncan finally shifted, his head rolling weakly to the side to stare at Ed. He released the hand he held and cupped Ed's chin. "I wish I could be normal, Ed."

"I don't need normal."

"I'll never be able to do what you want."

Ed stroked the jaw in his palm with a thumb. He was beginning to understand that, and why. "If you wanted to stay, I'd never let you go," Ed said, meaning it.

Resignation darkened Duncan's gaze. "This is what I tried to warn you about. I don't do relationships. I'm the last person you should want. I'm no good for anyone."

Ed knew that wasn't true, at all. He also knew Duncan wasn't going to believe anything different.

Battling his feelings, even when he knew he couldn't win, he asked, "Do you want to stay for tonight? We are friends, and if that's all there is, then…" Ed wouldn't press, but he could see fatigue in Duncan's posture. One long day, for the both of them. After his parents' and then tonight, he was toast. He was sure Duncan was as worn.

A quick hunt into the corner showed Margo watching, apparently picking up on Duncan's tension but as well-trained as Ed knew she was, she didn't break her command. She wagged her tail when Ed caught her stare to let them know she was paying attention if she was needed.

Duncan seemed uncertain when Ed faced him once more.

"Do you really want to drive back two hours right this minute?" Ed cajoled.

His mouth hiked up at the corner. "Frankly, no."

"Then go use the bathroom first. It's way too small to share. Do you want something to sleep in?"

"I'll be okay in my skivvies."

Ed stroked Duncan's cheek with the backside of his fingers. There was a raw rasp brought on by the growth of late day stubble. Ed swallowed the sigh. He wanted to lick the curve of Duncan's jaw to feel it. He redirected his thoughts. "It's okay. I will miss you, though."

"You're a great guy, Ed. I mean that."

Ed tried to smile. It wasn't until Duncan had risen and vanished into the bathroom that he went boneless against the couch. Just his fucking luck. The last thing he wanted was to have his heart broken. Looked like he didn't have a choice in the matter.

* * * *

Ed flipped on the couch staring at shadows as they did a silent dance over the ceiling. He'd waited until he was sure Duncan had relaxed on the bed and was comfortable before following him to get cleaned up. When he didn't go behind him into bed, he didn't know if Duncan had been aware, or if he'd already been drifting into sleep. Sharing the bed made certain things too tempting so Ed had put himself on the couch if for nothing else, to keep his sanity. He wasn't going to torture himself over Duncan.

Too late. He rubbed eyes that refused to close and dug his shoulders into the couch, determined to get comfortable.

A shadow that didn't belong moved into his vision. Ed didn't have to look twice.

"That looks as comfortable as laying on rocks."

Ed shifted his legs again, the couch too short for his length. "Go back to bed, Duncan." He sighed, trying to rein in the growl. Ed wasn't brimming with patience at the moment. He blocked the sight of the other man with an arm over his eyes. He wasn't made of steel, and Duncan was standing in his bedroom doorway, silhouetted and gorgeous. Bare-chested and with long, muscled legs. After making his case clear, Ed really didn't know why he was there, fixating on him.

Duncan could prove exactly how weak Ed was if he didn't get his ass back into that bedroom.

A light touch skimmed up his inner calf, along his knee to travel up his inner thigh. His breath hitched and he fought the urges that caress shot through him.

"Duncan." This time the growl was clear and intended. He was fighting—them, him, everything—and losing. His dick was waking up no matter how hard he fought. He hoped at least in the dimness it wasn't blatantly obvious.

He flipped to face the back of the couch, dislodging Duncan's lingering stroke.

"That's not exactly a bad view," Duncan teased.

Ed shot off the couch to his feet. "What do you want from me?" He paced around the other man. He couldn't bring himself to look right at Duncan. It was torture any way he sliced it. "I accepted your limits, I wasn't going to push. Then you call me out of the blue, and remind me about all the things I liked about you to begin with. You were even great with my mom." He shoved a hand through his hair, shaking as he warred against the boiling attraction. "I need more, Duncan."

He needed to know he was needed, that he could be what Duncan needed, too. He craved the connection that he knew Duncan wasn't going to allow. And Duncan was driving him to his limits, and right over them, with barely more than a few words.

"And this is bad, right now?"

With his back to Duncan, Ed shrugged his shoulders feeling the weight of the world on them. "No, it's unbelievable, and that makes it that much harder to stay away from you." He'd never been weak over a man, but Duncan was breaking him.

Duncan's body heat flanked him, until Ed knew exactly where he was, felt him through every pore without seeing him at all. He bit his lip to not growl again. He'd invited Duncan to stay, only because he didn't want him driving tired. *Liar, liar.* He'd deal with that later.

"I had a nightmare."

Ed spun on a dime, gazing into troubled eyes. "A bad one?"

"There are no good nightmares," Duncan pointed out. "Talking about what happened probably loosened the gates."

Ed cradled Duncan's jaw with his palms. Dark lashes lowered and the grooves cutting into his brow that he hadn't really seen in the darkness until then, softened.

"How can I help?"

"Come to bed. That's all I'm asking. Not swearing to staying innocent, but that's all I'm asking for."

"I don't think I can."

Duncan swallowed, looking away in clear dejection. "I understand. I told you I was damaged, Ed."

Ed forced him straight to stare into pain shadowed eyes. Stroking over his bottom lip with the pad of a thumb, he said, "I don't think I can stay innocent."

And like a drug, Ed was pulling Duncan into a fierce kiss, unable to stop the craving.

Chapter Fifteen

Duncan moaned, reaching upward with rough fingers to grip at Ed's hair. He braced the other man's waist with his naked arm and Ed growled, low and hungry, grinding their groins together. At least now the pounding of his heart was for something he wanted.

He'd been disoriented for several minutes after jerking upright in bed. He wasn't at home and nothing had been familiar. The walls were too close, the room too still. Then he'd realized he was alone. With a shiver of fading sounds and memories, he'd slid from the bed in search of Ed. He hadn't been sure what to make of finding him on the couch. Had his dreams driven him from the bed?

Before he could stop himself, he'd crossed the short space and touched exposed skin, and everything else ceased to matter. He needed Ed back in that bed, or he wouldn't sleep a second more.

He knew he was asking a lot of Ed right then, drowning in the assault of Ed's kiss. He was asking for more than he could give in return. Chris' warning returned. Even Ed's ex knew Duncan was using Ed, and he hated himself for it, for knowing he was doing it. Using him to push away the heat, the grit, and the pain haunting him. Ed needed an equal partnership. He'd made that clear. Knowing he was being a bigger dick with every second by greedily taking what Ed would give him made him clench his fingers that much harder.

Duncan wasn't whole. His mind and soul were riddled with Swiss cheese holes. The nightmares and memories would always be there, stalking him, waiting for a weak moment to return, asleep or awake. Ed deserved someone who could give him what he needed, a man who was, if not perfect, at least whole, because Duncan knew he couldn't give Ed either of those things.

He'd never been able to let anyone in. There was no one he'd ever met to make him think twice about giving that power to another. Not in his youth, not in the military. He could follow orders but couldn't share himself. He would never know someone deep enough to love them, to have their love in return. He'd accepted that wouldn't change. He didn't want it to, and never had a desire or a reason to try to make himself change.

Trouble had been his middle name since the beginning. He'd grown up knowing he was a handful. His own mother hadn't wanted him. He didn't care about not having a father he'd never known existed. He'd challenged authority, deflected anyone who dared to get close. How many times had he stood before a judge waiting for the ultimate punishment for exactly those offenses? He hadn't lied when he'd said it had been the military or jail. He'd rammed that line for almost three years when the last warning came. He'd enlisted the day he'd turned eighteen and hit boot camp three days after graduation. There had been no other avenue for him then.

Ed released his lips and tipped his chin, biting with painful tugs to the underside of Duncan's jaw making his knees shake. Fingers gripping at short brown hair clutched in reaction. Those bites were definitely bringing his focus to the man currently gnawing on him. Goose bumps flared over his chest as those sharp teeth delivered shocks to nerves. With his head arched to a near painful angle, rough fingers teased and pinched hardened flesh.

Ed sucked up bruises on Duncan's chest. A firm push moved them, directing his feet he didn't care where. A moment later, the bed hit his legs. The heat from Ed's mouth didn't change, roaming his chest to bite and suck, then lick with driving need. As Ed sank slowly downward to the floor in front of him, he dragged Duncan's drawers with him, giving his erection room to rise up and slap his stomach before bobbing to rest in front of him.

Ed didn't speak, merely giving a rough hum of approval before sliding the crown between his lips. Duncan didn't want words. He wanted to go to some place out of his own head. He stretched out his legs, and Ed jumped on the opportunity. Stars sparked across his vision when a hand firmly grasped and tugged at his balls. He thrust his length into Ed's wet heat and the man took it.

"Fuck," he growled, watching Ed's mouth go wide to take his cock. A current rocked his spine when the intensity on his balls increased. He flattened his palm to the back of Ed's head, grinding his teeth to not come.

A single, sharp tap to his sac jerked him straight. Ed popped off his dick. "Don't you fucking come." He kissed the place he'd teasingly stung. "On the bed."

Trembling he was so hard, it was about all he could do to fall backward and center himself on the mattress.

A naked Ed clambered up after him and settled between his knees. Duncan simply watched him this time, trusting him. He wasn't wrong to put that trust in him when that hot mouth went to work on his nuts. He widened willingly and let Ed put him where he wished. It worked to both their benefits. Desperately, he grabbed at the bed as Ed continued the assault. Duncan's heart pounded. Blood pulsed with volcanic force.

Ed scrambled his brain with his next move. He shouted at the firm nip and lick to flesh that had never known the sensation. "Fucking hell! What—" It was impossible to unclench his jaw to talk. Reflexively, he pressed into the stroke, the jab at his entrance that released a fireball into his blood. He hissed in a long stream. "Ed!" He couldn't count the number of times he'd rimmed a partner, thriving in the thrill it delivered. *Fuck.* He felt ready to explode.

The man didn't relent and Duncan couldn't fight the need. He gripped his dick and fisted his engorged cock with blinding speed.

His spine snapped and he came, shooting high across his chest. Ed's grunt followed right after. His shoulders bunched and heaved as he found his own release. He sagged to rest on Duncan's thigh, his hot breath panting over wet, sensitive flesh.

It was several minutes before either moved. Ed stumbled from the end of the bed. Duncan heard the water then the quick swipe of cloth over his chest.

Ed finished cleaning everything and returned, crawling into the bed and hefting Duncan into his chest. "Sleep now," he offered gently. A single kiss on Duncan's shoulder was the last thing he felt before he lost the battle for consciousness.

* * * *

Duncan twitched in his sleep. Heat seared his nostrils. Sand blew in gritty waves on gusts of wind. Fucking sand got into everything. He blinked, fighting the glare. It wasn't even the hottest point of the day and he felt like he was walking through an oven. The weight of gear and layers of salt and sweat-stiffened uniform added to the oppressiveness. His rifle was held at the ready in his hands, all his senses alert. Like clockwork, the team moved forward, the entire scene so deeply entrenched in his memory, he couldn't escape it.

Duncan's chest began to burn with the race of his heart. He knew what was coming, and fought to stop it. Tried to warn the men in front of him. He couldn't move, couldn't speak. The tragedy of dreams.

Gunfire erupted. Pockets of dust and debris popped from the surrounding ground and walls as bullets shattered the world around him in eerie slow motion. His shoulders tensed as he fell against the building at his back. Time stopped and skipped—the evil mechanizations of a splintered memory. He knew what was coming and inside, tried to wake from it, but it was wasted energy. Fighting their attackers, exposed as they tried to find cover, the first rocket exploded and he screamed in his sleep, shooting awake. Gasping, sweating, and panting, he clutched the covers. A flash of light made him flinch. The burst was immediately followed by a clap of thunder so intense it rattled the windows to gradually fade to a rumble.

He raked his hand down his face. Ever so slowly, his heart slid back into place behind his ribs. The storm raged on overhead, light so bright he had to close his eyes as lightning split the skies. The thunder... The raw power of the thunder chilled his skin. Rolling enough on the bed to reach the handle, he yanked open the drawer next to its edge and palmed the little zipper bag filled with earplugs. He managed to block his ears before the next round split the night in half.

He could feel it where his hair stood on end, from the static electricity bouncing in the air. The shock wave disturbances those powerful rumbles created. He could suffer those with the sound muted. He sat on the bed and curled his arms around his knees, wrapping caging fingers over the opposite arm like a bracelet. With his eyes closed, he counted, focusing on the gaps of seconds, if that long, between bursts and explosive response.

As the storm moved on and faded, so did Duncan's tension. His shoulders ached from the hold he'd maintained.

While sweat cooled across his bare chest, he slit his eyes to study the empty side of the bed. He had said his last goodbye to Ed almost three weeks ago. Not even a shared breakfast. He'd gathered and left. End of story. The dreams had grown vicious in their resurgence, making him a bigger wreck than usual. He wanted to blame Ed's poking, making him relive those moments, but he knew he was lying to himself.

If he were being honest, he had never slept as well as he had as when he was held in Ed's muscled arms, either before or after. Ed kept the demons at bay every time. For the first time in Duncan's life, he wanted someone. He missed the other man. When he knew he didn't deserve him after the way Duncan had treated him, dismissed him; for the first time in his life, he wished. The truth twisted his gut and he shied away from it. He wasn't ready to accept the possibility or face it.

Duncan couldn't remember the name of any particular hookup he'd had overseas. Half the time, he'd never even asked their names. It was a mutual anonymity. He understood that. Under Don't Ask, Don't Tell, the wrong word to the wrong person would see your ass discharged with little warning and no apology. That was gone now, but it had held a stranglehold on him and those like him during his tours.

As the storms within and outside abated, he cupped his head, bracing his stump to his cheekbone, missing the comfort, the known flesh feel of his own palm. He couldn't hold it there for long. Pressure on the end made it throb. A plate had been molded and screwed to the bones, giving him the needed anchor socket while allowing him muscle controlled flexing ability. The electrodes spaced intermittently under the skin helped to give him mobility control to his attachment, but it would never be the same. Would never feel the same.

And Ed hadn't cared one bit about any of it.

A slow breath shuddered through his body when that thought marched through his mind. Duncan had to give the man props. Ed had never once acted like Duncan was a case to be dealt with. He'd seen the shock in Ed's eyes that first afternoon when he'd bared it to him in the firehouse parking lot. Right then, he'd immediately thrown him into the bucket with every other jerkwad who'd treated him like shit because of his hand when Ed had stumbled over his words and couldn't string two together.

He huffed with a derisive sound aimed purely at himself. Chris had nailed it soundly. The only person who had—*still had*—a problem with his hand was Duncan himself. Ed had proven he didn't. Surprise was one thing. Surprise wasn't disgust. Duncan knew that. He shouldn't have been as quick to judge, either.

Through it all, Ed had grown on him. Duncan swallowed slowly when it hit him that he *liked* Ed. The one thing he'd never allowed, Ed had accomplished—he'd gotten under Duncan's skin.

With a glance at the clock, he readily accepted he wasn't capable of enough coherent thought to do something about it at three in the morning. Discovering the thunder had rolled well off into the distance, he twisted the foam plugs out of his ears and dropped them onto the nightstand beside the bag.

A little more relaxed, but no less confused to his desires and future, he slunk onto the bed beneath the covers, tucking them up around his chin. He glanced toward Margo, who lay watching him from her crate.

"It's okay, girl. I'm okay."

A shallow tail thump was followed by a good stretch. Her vigil completed, she closed her eyes and fell asleep.

Duncan wished his sleep were as easy to find.

Chapter Sixteen

Another week passed and Duncan started to get a clue. He wasn't okay. He was sleeping for shit. Two more nights of autumn storms had put him in such a black mood, even Margo was beginning to walk on eggshells around him and he'd never hurt a hair on her body. He had to bite his tongue to not snap at every little shadow and sound. Lack of sleep caused by nightmares was draining him. He knew how he could at least calm his mental specters if he couldn't get rid of them.

Except... He couldn't bring himself to be reliant on anyone. It burned to know that anyone had that effect on him. That any person could get so deep under his skin.

Margo approached him where he stretched out on his chair. She patiently rested her chin on his thigh and he scratched behind her ears. She was trying to make him feel better. He knew that. Further proof of how messed up he was getting, and the last thing he wanted to do was go see his shrink over it.

"What should I do, girl?" he mused out loud.

Brown eyes swept up to stare at him from the lethargic calm he'd put her into with the scratches.

Duncan knew he didn't have any right to ask Ed for anything after their last night together. He'd made it clear he couldn't go further with him. The man needed something he'd had never given another.

Duncan really didn't know if he even could. If he could be that…*vulnerable*.

He drifted to let his head rest on the chair with his eyes closing. Eventually, Margo slid away to lie down, leaving him alone in his thoughts.

He kept hoping that everything would go back to the way it had all been. Before. Whatever that was.

The last thing he was expecting to get was a call from Ed. He stared at the ID on the phone as it rang, his stomach immediately going into knots. So many reasons the man would be calling. A thousand more he shouldn't be at all.

"Hello?"

"It's me," Ed said, his voice croaky and raw.

"Hey, man. You okay?" Duncan sat up in the chair, both feet on the floor. His senses were tingling. Something was very wrong. In an instant, all the mental arguing vanished.

"I— Fuck. I need a friend."

Duncan nodded. "I'm always that," he said earnestly.

"Can you meet me in Stiller Springs, at the hospital?"

"What happened?" He was already pushing himself up before he spoke, taking long strides to reach his room and clean up.

"Mom had a stroke this morning."

"Fuck," he choked out in utter shock. He didn't know Ed's parents well, but he did know they were good people.

"Dad called while I was on shift, and I didn't find out until I got the messages here." Ed took a steadying breath. "Terry gave me leave."

"Stay there. I'll pick you up. You're not in any shape to drive."

"It's out of your way," Ed argued.

"Stay there, Ed." Duncan swallowed. "Please?" The fear of Ed being too out of it and having a wreck terrified him. Suddenly, nothing mattered but being there for him. It didn't matter how they'd left things last time. It didn't matter that his world had been one massive knot since that night. Ed was his only worry. "I'll be there as quick as I can. I'll have my phone."

A shuddered breath on the other end told him Ed was trying to get his shit together.

"Thanks."

"No problem. I mean that. Let me get changed and I'll hit the road."

Another quick goodbye and Duncan let him go. The next call he made was to the kennel where he took Margo for play dates or grooming. He arranged for an overnight stay. With that set up, he was in and out of the shower in two minutes, forgoing the razor.

It took him a good half an hour to get out of the house and then to drop off Margo. He knew he had been speeding when he cut nearly fifteen minutes from his usual drive time. He didn't even have to get out of the truck when he pulled to a stop in front of Ed's door. The man was already on his way out to meet him.

A nod in greeting once he was in the truck and Duncan left Silo. Ed's features were drawn and pale as he sat stiffly on his side of the cab.

"Is she okay?"

"For the moment. They're determining the damage the stroke caused."

"Why did he call the house phone?" Duncan asked.

Ed stared out the window, his gaze blank. "We were doing maintenance this morning and I didn't have my cell on me."

Now Duncan understood that tone. He was blaming himself for missing the calls. Duncan knew Ed wouldn't listen right then, but he wasn't going to let him believe that for long. The drive was tense, the truck's interior filled with Ed's worry.

Duncan stayed at Ed's side as they entered the hospital and went up a floor to find Ed's father. He kept his focus on Ed to escape the shudders being in those blandly utilitarian halls created. Hospitals ranked at the bottom of places he wanted to see. He'd seen enough of them to last his entire lifetime.

"Dad?"

They approached the silver-haired man bent over his lap sitting on the waiting area chair. His father looked up and stood. Duncan's chest tightened at the pain in the man's eyes. This was not going to be good.

* * * *

Ed reached his dad and engulfed him in a hug. "How is she?"

"They're running tests."

After a fierce squeeze, Ed stepped back. "You remember Duncan?"

"I do." They shook hands.

"Why don't you sit, Mr. Norwood. I'll find some coffee."

"Thanks, Duncan," Ed's dad replied hollowly.

Ed watched Duncan spin and aim for a station, then he eased into a chair beside his dad. "Did they say what caused it?"

Kent bowed his head, holding clutched hands over his lap. "Couple of things. Her blood pressure hasn't been good lately. The Alzheimer's seemed to have stabilized, but I didn't realize she was skipping medications because of it."

Ed closed his eyes and swallowed the sob. He knew he should've been there. "I'm so sorry, Dad."

A hand stroked his back. "Not your fault." Kent sat straight. "I'm the one who wanted to keep her home."

"What?" Ed blinked, clearing damp vision.

"The doctor wanted to give her a home care evaluation two months ago." Kent looked away, his face sheet white.

"Why didn't you?" *Why didn't you tell me?*

"I thought I could take care of her. I'm retiring at the end of the year. I'd be there for her." He gushed a harsh breath. "I wasn't ready to admit we're getting old."

"Dad." Ed choked up, his throat raw from the intensity of withholding his emotions. How could he have missed this?

"Here you go."

Ed's gaze traveled up lean legs and found Duncan holding out three small cups. Ed grasped two. "Thanks. Take it, Dad." Numbly, his father palmed the offered cup.

"Thank you, Duncan."

"Welcome," he offered. Duncan sat at Ed's shoulder on his other side.

"When will they update you?" Ed sipped though he tasted nothing.

"Should be soon."

What he hadn't expected was to feel Duncan's arm slide over his thigh. He reached for the fake hand and clasped it. Duncan's next breath warmed his ear when he exhaled.

"I'm here for you."

Ed gave him a watery smile and settled in to wait with his dad.

The wait felt interminable. Endless. Like time stood still in that pocket of circled chairs and plain walls. The TV in the corner was on some news station with the volume turned down. More reports of the coming cold weather. It was a pointless distraction. It did nothing to stop the recriminations. He should have known. Should have seen something.

Ed repeatedly went over the conversations he'd had with his parents, the visits since that time he'd introduced Duncan to them. His father had hinted at nothing. Now it was almost Thanksgiving.

"How did she go downhill so fast?" Ed asked, gazing sideways at his tired father.

"I lied," his father gruffly divulged. "I wasn't ready to let her go into someone else's care and I knew if you knew how bad her condition was, you'd push for the doctor's side."

"I wouldn't have," Ed argued, but his dad put a hand to his knee and gave him a good squeeze.

"Yes, you would have, because it would have been the right thing to do. She needs real care."

Ed sipped at his cooling coffee to hide the lump in his throat. He understood his father's reluctance to explain, but it still hurt that he'd been kept in the dark.

"I didn't tell you any of this because I wanted to get through Christmas, but I've been looking into taking her south. She needs warmer weather."

"You're leaving?" Ed jerked in his chair. It felt like he'd been slapped.

His father wouldn't meet his gaze. "I was going to tell you over Thanksgiving, give you a chance to get used to the idea, but after this…" Kent sighed, groaned really. "Originally, we'd discussed relocating next summer. Now, if the doctor's say it's safe, we'll be leaving by February."

"Fuck!" Ed lurched to his feet and stalked down the hall. He found a bin and threw his coffee into it. His stomach was on the verge of losing everything in it. The coffee wasn't helping.

He stood at the end of the long hall with his hands clenching, hidden in his light jacket pockets while he battled inside. He couldn't believe his father would make these kinds of decisions without letting him know *something*. He was silently staring out a window at nothing when the strength of a single arm wound around his middle beneath his crooked elbow.

"He still loves you," Duncan whispered over his shoulder.

"I know. Just…" He released a harsh breath. "All at once." It felt like he'd collided with a two ton boulder and was left flat in its wake. He couldn't think of when he'd been more gutted.

"I don't doubt it." Slowly Duncan eased around his frame to face him. "But it also tells me, he wants to do this. He's a strong man, like his son. He takes care of those he loves. It may not sound like it, but he was also thinking of you."

Ed huffed. "By not telling me how bad things had gotten?" He doubted that.

"No, well, partially maybe. But he was already planning on how to do this so it wouldn't hurt you more than it had to. He wanted to give you time to understand his reasoning, but his plans have changed now."

Ed finally relented and sagged forward to brace his forehead on a strong shoulder. He didn't know what to think. Getting the message from his dad earlier that day had already set the tone for the following hours. He was in shock and he knew it.

Winding his arms around Duncan, he held him close. "Thank you."

"Here for you, man," Duncan said, nuzzling under his ear. Soft lips caressed his neck then Duncan stood straight.

Ed could have stayed like that for hours, but knew it wasn't an option. "We better get back. He's going to need us tonight. Will you stay?"

Duncan leaned close and brushed a kiss to Ed's lips. "As long as you need me."

Releasing him and turning around to plod in the other direction, Ed asked, "Where's Margo?"

"With the sitter. She'll be fine until I get home."

The last thing Ed expected was for Duncan to thread their fingers together on the walk down the hall. He didn't take them back, either, when Kent spotted them. Ed took that strength and wrapped himself into it. He knew in the coming hours he was going to need as much as he could get.

Chapter Seventeen

Duncan was driving Ed home for the night and would likely stay with him for the next day, if not longer. Ed slouched on the seat in the truck beside him. Quiet snores proved the day had caught up with him. Duncan would stay as long as he could. That way they could relieve Ed's dad and let him take a break if he wanted in the morning. The hospital had placed a bed in his wife's room for Kent and he'd sent Ed home for the night. Ed hadn't wanted to leave, but even Duncan knew he wasn't helping.

The prognosis was favorable that Ed's mom would regain a lot of her mobility, but now there was no doubt. His mother would need home care, at least for the foreseeable future.

Duncan turned up the heater a little to keep Ed from getting chilled while he rested. It was a guilty pleasure to sneak peeks at the man when he was asleep and unaware. The strain of the day had washed away with the sleep, leaving his color warmer and the tight lines around his mouth smoothed out.

Duncan's own tumultuous thoughts and worries of earlier that day had faded to take care of Ed's needs first. Ed was giving him focus. He honestly wished it had been for a better reason.

Stopped at an intersection, he reached over and flipped through hair that had grown past Ed's ears.

Ed sighed in his sleep. It echoed almost like longing within Duncan's center.

It was only a little longer before he was at the drive in front of the house to Ed's rented apartment. "Ed, we're here." He put the truck into park and stopped the engine.

Lashes fluttered as Ed blinked, clearing his vision with hard palm scrubs. Brown eyes in a pale face rolled toward him, blank, bloodshot, and a little glassy. Duncan cupped the other man's chin and drew him close. It wasn't a fierce kiss. He couldn't remember a kiss that hadn't been fueled by a need for sex.

This was his first. Soft and caring. Comforting. Duncan never knew he had it in him. He was panting when he let Ed go, shocked at the rush of feeling that heated his veins. It wasn't even arousal so much as something deeper. He cleared his throat and said, "Let's get inside. It's late."

Ed nodded and sluggishly unbuckled his belt to slip from the truck. Duncan walked a pace behind him until both were inside. Ed hung up his jacket and Duncan did the same.

"Do you want me to make you something to eat?" Duncan offered. He doubted Ed had eaten much of anything all day.

"Thanks, but maybe in the morning. Drained. You want the bathroom first?"

"No, go ahead. Take your time."

Ed stripped on the way, clothes falling without care. The quiet click of the bathroom door told Duncan he wanted to be alone. He didn't push it. He undressed while waiting for Ed to finish. The last thing he had to do was remove the attachment and wash his arm. He studied the thin scars that appeared from the edge of the attachment sleeve, reaching in snaking patterns for his elbow. Some were reconstruction sutures while others were burn damage and healed slices. He had a matching arrangement that reached from his ribs, over his left hip, and well down his thigh, all reminders of the blast he couldn't physically remember. It was with dawning realization that Ed had never made an issue out of any of them. Didn't plague him with questions, didn't constantly focus on them when they were together. As if they were simply a part of him. The truth tightened Duncan's throat until he swallowed to control it.

The bathroom door popped open to a billowing cloud of steam. "There's a toothbrush and clean towels."

"Thanks, sexy," Duncan offered gratefully. "Keep a spot warm for me."

Ed chuckled, right until Duncan smacked his cotton-covered ass with a sound swat. "Ouch!"

Duncan hopped out of arm's reach, smiling when he heard Ed's grumbles. He couldn't help himself. Being around the bigger guy had put his libido back into play. One look from those brown eyes, one sweet touch, and Duncan was craving. He wanted to tussle and roll around like dogs on that bed.

Shutting the door, he shook his head, hiding his groan. *He's killing me. Why can't I get him out of my head?* The problems he'd been drowning in just that morning were still there, and he wasn't any closer to finding answers.

After removing his attachment, he opted for a quick shower. Teeth brushed and hair almost tamed, he rejoined Ed in the bedroom. He found the other man lying on his back, staring up at the ceiling with his hands palmed behind his head.

Duncan slid under the covers. "One day at a time," he offered, rubbing a soothing hand over Ed's chest. He'd gotten into the habit of sleeping where his right hand was free to touch, and that was something he'd never get tired of doing, not to Ed. The man was nothing but solid.

"I know. I'm worried about Dad now, too. Can he handle all of Mom's care?"

"He won't have to," Duncan said. "She's going to get good home care from a center he's already researched. He'll be there for her, but he won't be doing it alone."

"Should I go with them?"

That stumped Duncan. Brown eyes blinked then gazed at him expectantly. "What about everything you've worked for here?"

Ed snorted. "What? My nearly nonexistent pay for being on call and working a hundred plus hours straight? Why do you think I rent this box? I was grateful the town chose me as one of their paid crew rather than as a volunteer. Now..." Ed shifted, digging his shoulders into the mattress. "I'm tired of being alone, Duncan," Ed admitted, then swallowed as a red hue fanned over his cheekbones. "Never mind." He flipped to a side, giving Duncan his back. "Let's get some sleep."

Duncan settled behind him, spooning them together sharing body heat. It wasn't as easy to find sleep with the possibility that Ed could follow his parents hanging like an unanswered question over them. Duncan didn't begrudge his relationship with them. After spending more time with Ed's father,

Duncan could easily see the closeness they shared. Kent loved his wife and son deeply.

Then why did the thought of Ed going with them leave Duncan unsettled and feeling hollow? What did he have to offer Ed? An occasional roll in the sack? After witnessing Kent's love for his wife, Duncan could also see why Ed felt the way he did. They were good role models to try to emulate. A partnership where people cared, stood by one another, supported each other even in need. When had Duncan ever had that in his life? One answer: Never.

Ed's slow breathing told him he'd drifted off held in his arms. It took a while, but eventually Duncan was able to follow him into a restless sleep himself.

* * * *

Duncan reached for his cell phone by his computer when it rang. Thanksgiving had passed and winter had set in with snow storms threatening not too far into their future. He and Ed had been trading phone calls almost daily since Judy's stroke. Even though both he and Ed had argued they were nothing but friends, Kent had continued to treat him more and more like family.

"Well, hello hot stuff," he growled. It warmed Duncan when he could hear Ed's smile, at least a small one considering all the stress he was now under.

"Are you busy this weekend?"

"Let me check my calendar." He paused for a scant heartbeat, then, "Let's see. I have to meet with the President, fly to Beijing, teach a cooking class, and then go build water pipelines in South Africa. That's Saturday," Duncan drawled.

"Har har." He dropped into a rough chuckle.

Duncan couldn't restrain his lips from twitching into a grin. It sounded good when Ed laughed. He hadn't done it much in the last month. "Why?"

"Want to go to a Christmas thing with me?"

"A party?" Duncan relaxed in his chair, running a gloved finger over his chin. It turned into a lazy scratch because he hadn't bothered to shave that morning.

"Chris and Jamie," Ed explained. "It's for the clinic crew, but they're inviting friends and hooligans."

"Like me?" Duncan joked. He was probably the only hooligan they knew.

"It's okay. I'll vouch for ya."

Duncan snickered. "Sure. Meet at your place?"

"Sounds good. You can bring Margo if she'll be okay here for a few hours."

"She should be fine," Duncan said.

"Cool. Get here before five on Saturday. I'll let Chris know you're coming. Oh, and dress warm."

They talked for a few minutes about Ed's mother, then Duncan let him go. At least he had something to look forward to in two days. Pushing away from the desk with Ed's words on his mind, he went to add a sweatshirt to stay warm under his coat so he could take Margo for a walk.

* * * *

Duncan usually had no reason to get into the Christmas spirit, but it looked like for at least the next few hours, he'd have no choice. At Chris and Jamie's house, twinkling lights had been strung from one end of the front to the other, as well as several yards' worth on fences and on the back paddock near the barn.

"Is that a tree?" Duncan pulled the truck up to join the other vehicles already there, shaking his head at the bedecked mass in the yard. He assumed it had at one time been a tree, but now it was buried in streamers, garlands, lights, and dozens of ornaments. Duncan didn't recall seeing it during his last visit, but then again, they'd been inside and behind the house. Studying the mishmash of decorations, he wondered if the kids Ed had mentioned on the way over had been the engineers of the masterpiece.

"Looks like it," Ed mused. "Come on."

They followed the noise of children's laughter to the rear of the house. A flat wagon with lights roped around the rails had been loaded with hay and Chris was lifting smaller children to helpful hands already onboard.

"That is a huge horse." Duncan gaped taking in the large animal.

"That's Tiberius. Chris does this every now and then. The kids love it." Ed nudged him with a shoulder. "Let's go see what the game plan is."

Clouds of steam rose from Tiberius as he stamped the ground. "Is he cold?"

"Impatient. He almost prances when he gets the harness on."

Duncan was amazed, watching the animal. He'd never been so close to a horse that big.

Ed must have noticed his stare. "Want to say hi?"

"To the horse?" Did horses that large eat people?

"Sure."

Ed's grin blossomed and Duncan's stomach did a funny somersault, making him feel a little wobbly inside. It had been weeks since Ed had looked so…happy. Duncan admitted, however silently, he'd missed that from him. Without the strain shadowing his features, the handsome man Duncan had grown to admire and call a friend made him crave to pull him close for a hard kiss, and maybe not stop with a mere kiss.

But then, what did that leave for him if Ed moved to help take care of his mother? Duncan didn't like the picture the absence of Ed in his life created. The wobbly sensation became a yawning pit as a future without Ed in it crystallized. He hadn't realized what the man's friendship had grown to mean to him. The question was, what was he going to do about it?

Following Ed dutifully, they stopped by the horse's side. "Let him sniff then pet his nose. It's super soft."

Duncan did as Ed suggested then laughed at the velvet softness. "Wow."

Ed captured his free hand in one of his before he could sneak it into a coat pocket and drew him to the end of the wagon. "Hey, Chris."

"Hi, guys. Want in on this one?"

Both Ed and Duncan studied the scrabbling children diving under blankets. "Next trip?" Ed asked.

Chris chuckled. "Don't blame you. There's a ton to drink and food inside. Help yourselves." Chris leaned close. "Santa will be by later for the kids." He winked, then reached for the step to climb onto the driver's seat. Hunting over his shoulder, he called, "Everyone set?"

A cheer of young voices and the calls of a few adults were clear. A snap of the reins and with a squeak of major proportions, the wagon and kids were moving. Tiberius tossed his head before he settled down into the easy plod of a work horse.

"He does the kids first, shoos them inside for hot chocolate then lets the adults cuddle up. It's actually kinda fun."

"Yeah?" Duncan's wistful breath became a broad cloud in the cold. The setting sun splashed an orange backdrop to the horizon through the haze of clouds in the distance. Duncan leaned close to Ed to share his secret. "Would it be awful to say I've never done it?"

Ed gave him a soft and quick kiss, the first of the night, and Duncan caught how unattached it was. Too sweet and far too calm. That would not do. He wanted the passion inside Ed. He jolted with those thoughts running wild inside because he didn't know when he'd realized he'd missed it.

A tug on his hand urged him to keep walking toward the house. "Then we will have to remedy that. Let's go warm up and wait our turn."

Ed was being attentive and kind, keeping him close, but watching the wagon move down the drive to the rise of singing voices, Duncan tried to figure out what was going through Ed's head. Maybe it was because there were so many little eyes to watch that he'd kept the kiss undemanding.

The thoughts of why it mattered and how he could change it hovered over him until they were inside and his focus was being pulled into a thousand other directions.

Chapter Eighteen

People milled about inside, laughing and shaking hands as they greeted Ed and Duncan walking into the house. The savory scents of holiday cooking, sugary desserts, hot chocolate, and the fruity-tangy pull of apple cider lured them through the house for the kitchen. Ed handed a mug of cider from the warming pot to Duncan once they could get close enough.

The man got better looking every time Ed saw him. He'd really become a good friend, a rock, over the last several weeks. When he'd needed to talk or have someone to take him out of his own head for a few minutes, he knew he could count on Duncan. His mom was home now and his dad had taken the rest of the year off, effectively initiating his retirement. Ed had driven to Stiller Springs nearly twice a week to visit them since his mother's stroke. He almost felt guilty that it had taken something so awful to happen before he realized he wasn't seeing them enough.

He kept hoping Duncan would come around, but more and more, it felt like a friend with benefits was the most Ed would be able to have with the man. *Whatever this is for the moment.* He needed something he didn't think Duncan would ever be able to give.

While he wouldn't stay solely for Duncan, the man added substance to his life in Silo. He did love his job. He loved his friends, but he had a duty to his parents that, as an only child, he couldn't ignore. His dad continuously argued that Ed didn't need to uproot his entire life because their health was determining their changes. But when they moved, they would no longer be an hour away, able to bring him home with a single phone call. He wasn't sure he was willing to let that happen.

"Penny for your thoughts?" Intense hazel eyes watched him over the rim of the mug in his hand. Steam wafted upward in lazy swirls. The fragrant cinnamon and apple aroma flirted with his stomach, making it want to rumble. When Ed couldn't find the words right away for more than one reason, Duncan leaned close. "Smile and have fun, sexy. Let it go for tonight."

Ed huffed then shook his head, his lips softening into a shallow grin. "How'd you know?"

"You get the cutest frown."

"I do not!" Ed denied quietly.

"Yes, you do." Duncan kissed his cheek.

"Oh, Mr. Fireman," came a jaunty call.

Ed blinked and swung to look the other direction. Jamie was smiling like he'd won the lottery.

"What, Trouble?"

Jamie pointed up. Ed hoped Duncan missed his quiet groan. "Seriously? Mistletoe?"

"Take a look." Jamie motioned toward the rest of the house with a palm. There were at least a dozen ribbon tied sprigs scattered throughout, hanging from the ceiling. It was a kissing minefield.

Duncan bit his lip to stifle his snickers.

Jamie put fists to hips. "Well?"

"Well, what?" Ed prompted, playing oblivious.

"Duncan, show the man what mistletoe is good for."

"My pleasure," he murmured right before he swung Ed around with a light but commanding press to his jaw.

Ed expected a peck on the lips. Honestly, they were in mixed company and there were still kids about, but none of that seemed to matter to Duncan. It started innocently enough. A playful caress of lips. Then Duncan urged him a hair closer while narrowing the distance chest to chest to apply a hint of carnal pressure. The tease of tongue made him hunger for a deeper sharing. Then he could taste the cider they'd been drinking when Duncan swept inside and circled his mouth with the heady strength of his tongue. Ed moaned, low and needy. It wasn't exactly a conflagration of fire, it was almost too languid for that, yet Ed burned when Duncan finally released him. He licked his lips, craving, his body yearning.

"Love kissing you," Duncan said, nuzzling him before letting him stand completely straight. Sharing in their own little world. Even his eyes sparkled.

Ed trembled. His heart dared to reach out for the man holding him. *Why can't I have you? Why won't you let me love you?* He bit his cheek to stay quiet, withdrawing from the spell of Duncan's lips, ready to glower at Jamie, only he was gone, mission accomplished.

"He did that on purpose," he grumbled.

"Regret it?" Duncan asked by his ear.

"No." Ed sighed. No, he didn't. He truthfully liked those kisses too much to be angry.

"Good, because I'm counting on taking advantage of the mistletoe as a reason to kiss you at every opportunity."

"Oh?" Ed slanted him a look. What was Duncan doing?

"Going to make you forget for at least tonight. Let the world go on without you for a few hours."

Heated currents wound over Ed's ear, causing flashes of need to shoot into his blood.

"The sexiest beast in this room." Duncan licked at an earlobe and Ed nearly sighed.

Oh, yeah. Duncan could definitely sway his decision to stay or leave. Duncan straightened and Ed was able to catch his breath, quietly wishing for the impossible.

Only... Duncan would never be more than a fuck buddy. He'd never let Ed take him, either. He'd never allow himself to open up to Ed's affections. He couldn't live like that. The pain that fact caused was unbelievable. To hide it, he turned to people watch, sipping at his drink to drown the lump in his throat. Duncan knew what Ed needed and had made it clear he couldn't and wouldn't go beyond his own limits. Friends. Sex. Nothing emotional. The emptiness that created within almost brought him to his knees.

Ed refused to settle on something this important. Not this time. He could bend, but Duncan had to try. He should walk away while he still could. Maybe following after his parents when they moved to Florida would be better all around.

It wasn't too much longer before a hoard of kids stampeded into the house hungry and cold, hunting for goodies and hot chocolate. Adults began unwrapping them from coats and scarves while they chattered with full enthusiasm about the ride and songs they'd sang.

"Come on," Jamie called, waving at Ed. "Our turn." He gave a wicked smile before vanishing for the back door, bundled up like an Eskimo. Ed could only guess what he had planned for Chris, and he was sure he didn't want to know.

"Still want to?" He found a safe place for his mug.

"I'm game," Duncan replied, copying him.

Ed found fingers and clasped them into his, drawing Duncan through the doorway for the yard once more.

Chris stood next to Tiberius, talking to him and feeding him carrots. A few couples were already ahead of them for the wagon ride. Ed smiled at Quade and a pretty redhead.

"There are plenty of blankets," Chris called, giving the horse's thick neck a final pat. Jamie clambered onto the high seat, fixing the blanket there. He watched Chris with so much love and devotion, Ed ached.

Looking up and away from them while giving the others a chance to get settled into the wagon, Ed became lost in the endless stars. "Something about a cold night and all that sky," he mused.

"It is something, isn't it?" Duncan offered, equally awed.

"Let's see if there are any good spots left." Reaching the edge, Ed counted four couples. "Still room?"

Quade shifted, huddling his date close between his legs. "A few inches," he teased.

Ed rolled his eyes and climbed up. Glancing behind, he made sure Duncan could manage before tugging on a blanket next to Quade and his date. When it popped free, Quade laughed deliberately.

"Smartass." Then Ed plunked down into the hay. Spreading his legs, he caught Duncan's wary gaze. "It's okay. No one cares."

Duncan neared and finally settled his rump between Ed's thighs. Ed tossed the blanket over them, pulling it around and tucking it down beneath. "Okay?"

Duncan nodded, resting his head on Ed's shoulder. "Never done this," he whispered.

Wisps of hair tickled Ed as they shifted on the mounds of prickly hay with the wagon wall behind them until they were comfortable. He loved Duncan's longer hair. He combed fingers through it to help put him at ease. "Relax. Seriously. Chris and Jamie are driving, and you know Quade." Ed curled his arms around Duncan and cradled him into his chest.

"You're actually cute together," Quade's date offered with a sweet smile. "I'm Maya."

"Nice to meet you," Ed answered, introducing himself and Duncan.

"Everyone set?" Chris called.

"Good to go," Quade replied, then burrowed into Maya's neck making her squeal in playful shock.

"Behave," she scolded.

An overdone grumble was louder than the creak of the wagon. "Party pooper."

Arching on his neck to stare upward, Ed lost himself in the stars as Chris got them in motion with a call to Tiberius. Those bright pinpoints of light somehow glistened brighter with the chill in the air, like ice. It was even better sharing that moment with Duncan in his arms. When Duncan skated fingertips over his hand under the blanket, he threaded their fingers together, winding them as tight as he could with their coats in the way.

"Warm enough?" Ed couldn't resist and nipped at an ear. It felt cold to his lips so he pressed his cheek to one and then the other to try to add some body heat.

Duncan moved restlessly, his butt scraping against Ed's groin. A low groan slipped out and Duncan tightened his hold on the fingers he held. "Feels good," Ed said as quietly as possible. Ed didn't want to let on what was being said or done, but he was ignoring as much as being ignored by the others focused on each other. Luckily the squeak and groan of the wagon hid a lot of other sounds, the hint of laughter, the murmur of voices. It wasn't just Ed and Duncan taking advantage of the semi-privacy of the heavy blankets.

The jostling of the wagon was aiding Duncan's teasing as well, turning Ed into a single nerve that sparked with every touch and squeeze. It was torture because they had to behave, but it was so good, their bodies bumping and nudging one another's. "You are so bad. A tease," Ed growled, keeping every word private.

Duncan twisted sideways with a shoulder into his chest, then nipped at the underside of Ed's jaw.

The sting made Ed want to throw the blanket over them completely and devour Duncan's mouth. The man was making keeping an emotional and physical distance impossible. Everything from the closeness Duncan was keeping to the kiss earlier was sucking Ed in.

They hadn't slept together since before his mother's stroke. There'd been comforting touches, a few supportive kisses, but until tonight, Ed had managed to keep a firm grip on his desires for the long-haired rebel. Duncan was pushing at him again, chipping away at his control, only this time he wasn't going to crack. He wasn't going to give in like the night of Duncan's nightmare. He'd wanted to help then and had expected nothing for the distraction to help Duncan sleep.

With his body wrapped around Duncan's to hold in heat against the frigid temperatures, he thought he was managing well enough to keep an emotional and mostly physical distance. He could maintain a wall between sex and everything else. For his sanity's sake, he had to.

Then Ed heard, "Don't leave."

He lurched to stare at a watchful Duncan. "What?"

Wide eyes awash in the stars overhead waited for him to fall into them, then closed briefly to reopen with attentive sharpness. Shadows flitting across Duncan's face were caused by more than the passing starlight.

Duncan tilted to sit as close as was possible into Ed's chest, to whisper into his ear. "I'm asking. Stay in Silo."

"Are you saying you want to give us a chance?" Ed was stock-still shocked, practically holding his breath. He hadn't expected anything of the sort and had been doing his best to protect himself from the disaster of falling for the man. This changed everything. Every single argument he'd held with himself that evening became so much dust—if he could believe in what he thought was being offered.

Duncan softened in Ed's embrace, his eyes becoming bold and luminous. "I think so," he replied, a mere wish away from Ed's ear.

A thousand questions flashed through his mind. Where had this come from? What had changed? Had anything? Why now? Was Duncan willing to meet him halfway? Ed didn't know where to start. The questions and all the possibilities made him dizzy. And not one could be discussed right then because he knew nothing would be an easy answer.

It appeared by his expressions and the tension still clinging to him, Duncan may have surprised himself, but he wasn't taking it back, either. Frustrated at the timing but relinquishing the immediate need to find out exactly what Duncan meant, he curled around Duncan's frame and tugged the blanket tight around them. "We'll talk later."

Duncan wound his arm over Ed's head and drew him close. Unlike the first light kiss of the evening, or even the sensually teasing kiss shared in the kitchen, this one went bone deep and spurred Ed into dreaming of plans for their future whether he wanted them or not.

Chapter Nineteen

Duncan's heart was pounding so hard, it was a wonder it wasn't heard over the crunching sound of the rolling wheels. He didn't know if he had the right to ask Ed to stay. He understood Ed's family, his mother, had to be a priority, but—and this was where it got tangled—Duncan wanted Ed. Wanted, craved, needed. The moment of clarity was so acute beneath the star-spattered sky, it had left him frozen where he'd stood on the wagon planks.

Ed thought he'd been uncertain about joining him under the blanket, two guys in a gathering of mixed couples.

He couldn't have been further from the truth.

It hit him then and there, rather soundly as he caught his balance on the wagon bed. Duncan didn't like the future he could see without Ed. He *liked* doing these things with him. Liked staking a claim to him in front of friends. Duncan wasn't a fool. He knew what Jamie's ploy had been as soon as he brought up the mistletoe, and he'd loved every second of that kiss. A shared blanket on a cold December night under the stars? When had he *ever* imagined he'd get the chance to do something so normal? Duncan never had. He'd always seen himself as alone. Ed was changing that.

The feelings, the moments he'd been dissecting for over a month now, made him uneasy. He'd lost sleep, and he knew the confusion had brought on more than one episode of nightmares, which seemed to be compounding the confusion.

Ed had done more than gotten under his skin. A friend, a lover, a confidant, supportive, and accepting. There was a simple and understanding patience in Ed.

Don't leave.

Closing his eyes to rest his forehead against the side of Ed's jaw, Duncan found something within his reach that could be his. Found someone who wanted *him* after a lifetime of being passed through the system, first CPS and foster homes right into the military. He'd always been invisible.

Since their initial meeting at the firehouse to help with the tornado searches, Ed had seen *him*. Had worried about him. Had cared, without knowing anything about him.

He was also admitting for the first time in his life that this was something he desperately wanted. The question remained of if he could be enough for Ed. He couldn't hide from that. Duncan knew Ed needed a stable and level playing field. Needed to have a man who could be vulnerable, open, trusting. Needed to know where he stood with his lover. That was only fair. For a man who hadn't ever dared traverse the ground of a relationship, Duncan understood that and didn't begrudge the hunk holding him that need.

Letting Ed down was his greatest fear now when he'd never feared anything. Laughed at life when challenges had cropped up. Sneered at authority until *he* decided the direction he was going to take. Everything up to then had been his choice. Which was probably why this thing with Ed was throwing him to the ground in a mental heap.

He'd made it clear he wouldn't and couldn't do a relationship. But...

The last thing Duncan wanted was to lose him. *Now if that isn't a kick in the balls.*

He clung a little closer when every cell of his being was urging him to run, to escape. Ed's embrace brought him that much tighter into his chest beneath their shared blanket as though the man holding him knew Duncan's internal struggle. Each breath Duncan drew against his neck was filled with the spice of clean skin. Ed's personal scent. Heady and male. When the truth had finally snaked its way into his being, he didn't know. When Ed had managed to carve a niche into his heart, Duncan couldn't say.

They needed to talk. He knew it. Fears he couldn't voice nipped at his heels. When he'd adamantly refused before, what if he tried now and he physically couldn't? He hadn't lied. Certain things triggered the PTSD. What if he was incapable? He wasn't sure he wanted to give that much of himself to anyone, if he was honest with himself, but it wasn't fair to Ed if he didn't at least try. Would he still have Ed's respect? Duncan shivered, his spine tense as he fought the silent battle.

"Shh," Ed whispered close to his ear. "You're thinking too hard. Relax. Leave it for a few hours." He nuzzled against Duncan's temple, repeating the same advice Duncan had offered earlier.

The rock and sway of the wagon as they rolled along beneath the starry sky continued to glide his frame against Ed's solid chest. Glancing up to find brown eyes watching him, muscles gradually loosened. The reward was Ed's smile.

He did the only thing he knew he could at that moment. He brought Ed close and kissed him until he could push away all the tumultuous thoughts plaguing him and enjoy the warmth of his kiss.

* * * *

"Okay, who wore their ugliest Christmas sweater?" Jamie called. "Line up! We have a prize for the best groaner!"

Ed pressed his laughter into Duncan's shoulder where he huddled in his arms before him. They'd dumped their coats with everyone else's in the spare bedroom and were currently enjoying the warmth of the house after the relaxing and almost too erotic hay ride. Kids were laughing while adults herded them around, keeping them from hitting the stack of treats nonstop. Ed was pretty sure it was a lost cause.

Jamie's call for contestants had everyone close in or pay attention. He and Duncan were comfortable and warm in the kitchen and had no intention of joining this game.

Seven adults, men and women, lined up in front of the tree. Ed winced at two in particular.

"Holy ugly wool," Duncan choked, rocking against Ed while trying to not to laugh too loudly at the array of unbelievable disasters. Glitter, one that had blinking lights, another with metallic garland and miniature bells. It was clearly going to be challenging to choose a winner.

Jamie waved to get everyone's attention "So, here we have it. Just remember, we have kids in the room, so keep it clean. Judging by noise, so choose your victim wisely." Jamie lined them up in front of the tall, lit Christmas tree.

"He's really going to do this, isn't he?" Duncan asked, tipped upward, close to an ear to keep it between them.

"He's a menace. I told you."

Jamie went down the line and got first names and one or two words to explain the sweater's story.

"Fringe? That is so eighties." Ed groaned through his laughter.

"But... But... It's *suede* fringe. That makes it classic," Duncan corrected him. Ed rocked them both the harder he laughed. "Did he say those were snowballs?" was for another.

"Some kind of balls," Ed remarked under his breath, apparently equally at odds over the white puffs sewn to the front in no pattern at all. "Snowman poop."

Duncan guffawed, swallowing his howls.

By the time Jamie hit the end of the line, everyone was dying with laughter.

"Okay. You had your chance to pick a favorite." He walked to the start of the line and raised a hand. The volume escalated with whistles, shouts and applause. He gave each person a few seconds to gain attention. One even waved her hands and egged on the crowd, earning an escalated cheer.

Ed heard, "Oh, man. If the drunk elves win..." Ed squeezed Duncan close. The caress of fingers over his clasped hands made his heart trip. He didn't know why Duncan was being openly physical, but he wasn't going to argue. It felt amazing, and they were having a good time. He wasn't going to fight the obvious.

A winner was eventually chosen and handed a small wrapped gift amid hugs and pats on the back.

A few minutes later, the clear sound of bells rang from outside the front door.

Jamie clapped his hands to get everyone's attention and then cupped an ear. "I do believe I hear Santa!"

The kids went spastic. A draft from the back door whipped through the house right before Chris joined them in the kitchen. "I see the house is still standing."

"Jamie's got them eating out of his hand," Ed remarked.

Chris smiled with sweet pride at his lover. "Somehow I figured he would." He took a hot mug someone handed to him with a thank you and drew a sip. "That hits the spot. I swear it dropped twenty degrees while I was bedding down the horses."

"Who'd you rope into playing Santa?"

Chris' eyes twinkled. "Who said I roped anyone? For all you know, it's really the jolly old elf."

Ed laughed warmly. A solid knock at the door drew Jamie to open it.

"Santa!" came a squeal of young, sugar-wired voices.

The production was streamlined and sweet. The red-suited fat man hunkered down with a large sack at his side and began calling up the kids one by one. They got candy canes with a small gift, and got to whisper their deepest wish.

Overall, it was one of the best parties Ed had ever been to. There were his friends, including many people of the community that he knew, if not deeply, at least by face and name. A few came to shake his hand, equally pleased to meet Duncan. Conversation was witty and lighthearted as everyone enjoyed the evening under Jamie's smiling care.

Don't leave.

Ed couldn't forget those two words as they danced through his thoughts whenever there was a quiet lag in the din. If he didn't leave to help his parents, if he stayed, would Duncan want to move to Silo to be with him? Was he being honest with wanting to give what they had a real shot? How much was Ed willing to bend? What about Duncan? He refused to force Duncan to do something he physically couldn't.

He dipped his head to rest against Duncan's. Ed knew how much he needed that balance, to share in the bond of sex. He really didn't know what he was going to do. He cared, almost too much.

No matter how hard he tried to protect himself, he was losing his heart to the man in his arms.

Chapter Twenty

Everyone started to give their goodbyes and thank yous to Chris and Jamie after Santa's departure. Parents wrangled children, stuffed them into coats, then offered hugs and holiday wishes. Slowly the house began to empty.

"Don't go yet," Chris had murmured before he joined Jamie to show their guests out. Ed and Duncan stayed in the kitchen, chowing down on more finger foods and hot drinks.

"I wonder who made all the food?" Duncan asked. "I could eat these stuffed bacon ball things for days." Humming in appreciation, he popped two more between his teeth then licked his fingers without apology.

"Did you smell the ham?" Ed shot back. "I think my stomach wanted the whole thing."

"Food. The fastest way to soothe the beast," Chris offered, joining them again. "Jamie did most of it. The cookies and fudge were brought."

"Where's Quade?" Ed asked, noting he seemed to be missing. Cade was nursing a beer where he leaned against cabinets, also waiting for whatever Chris wanted to share.

"He took his date home. Just wanted to invite you guys for breakfast in the morning without everyone else hearing. It's Christmas Eve and we both wanted to have family over."

Ed saw Duncan swallow hard to quickly sip at his mug. It seemed the offer of being included took him by surprise.

"After all of this?" Ed queried, meaning the chaos of the evening.

"This was easy."

"Says you," Jamie said, hip bumping Chris when he joined them. "You didn't slave in this kitchen for two days straight putting all of this together."

"And look how wonderful it came out," Chris said soothingly. "I'd have eaten my way through it if I'd been any kind of help at all."

Jamie crossed his arms but didn't deny it.

"You did good, baby." Chris kissed him and Jamie sniffed, softening marginally.

"Okay, you're off the hook. So who's coming in the morning? Quade's coming with Maya. Cade?" He nodded in answer. "Not that I've ever seen you two pass up food," Jamie pointed out.

Cade blinked in faked insult.

Ed jammed a cracker into his mouth to not laugh, because Jamie was right. The twins could eat their way through a buffet and scrape the bowls clean.

"He's got a mouth, Chris," Cade growled.

"Poor baby. She still hasn't called you back?" Jamie asked in sympathy.

Cade didn't answer, instead sucking hard on the bottle in his grip.

"Don't poke the bear," Chris admonished.

Cade sighed. "It's okay. I know he's just trying to make me smile." He pinched his lips together into a tight grimace. "There."

Jamie fearlessly jabbed a finger into Cade's ribs. "Laugh, damn you."

"Stop." Cade tried to scrunch his side, blocking with an elbow to avoid the offending finger.

"Not until you smile, damn it." The finger kept digging all the while Cade tried hopping out of range.

"Okay! Okay, uncle." He chuckled. "Finger of death," he griped.

"*High-ya!*" Jamie cried quietly, brandishing said finger toward Cade's ribs like a sword, fancy footwork included. Cade slid across the kitchen to stand out of reach behind Ed.

"Not protecting you, man," Ed warned.

"So, ten tomorrow good for you?" Chris asked, hooking Jamie's waist with a finger and tugging him into his body to keep him away from Cade. Ed heard the exhale of relief behind him.

"Ten sounds good to me." He glanced to Duncan who shrugged. "Oh, we have Margo," Ed mentioned.

"Bring her, too," Chris offered. "She's welcome."

"Bring an appetite. I have plans for the rest of the ham. And yes, I saw you eyeballing it, Ed." Jamie wiggled in contentment against Chris' frame. "This was a good night." He tipped to gaze up at Chris. "Thanks for doing it."

"Anything for you."

"Okay, I'm outta here before the mushiness flows unchecked." Cade finished his beer and dropped it in the recycle bin. He went around the bend and reappeared with a jacket in his hands. He tugged it over his shoulders. "See you in the morning."

"Drive safe," Chris offered, well-meant and caring.

"He's miserable," Jamie said as soon as the door closed behind him.

"Can't do anything about it." Chris glanced toward the door, then to Jamie.

"Girl problems?" Ed asked, getting another round of cider. He didn't know what Jamie did to the stuff, but it was the best he could remember.

"Unfortunately. He'll be okay."

"It was seeing Quade with Maya. He always thought he'd get his first," Jamie told them.

"How do you figure that?" Ed asked. He leaned against the counter and silently cheered when Duncan took up post next to him, shoulder to shoulder. It felt…nice. Like they were together. What made him even happier was Duncan wasn't shy about making that clear.

"Cade might look like a badass, but he's the smartest out of all three of us."

"It's the long hair," Ed joked, pulling on Duncan's strands with teasing flair.

"Jackass," Duncan muttered without heat.

"And they're competitive as hell, in everything," Chris added. "Why do you think Cade has the business degree? He had to do more than Quade."

"That's why? Really?" Jamie seemed positively stunned.

"Really." Chris scooped him into his arms. "He drove himself to have better grades, finish sooner. It's why when they argue, I don't get between them."

"Must have been rough growing up," Duncan mused.

"And then some," Chris agreed.

Duncan gave Ed a slight nudge and he gulped the last of his cider. "Okay, we're going to cut out," Ed told them. He put his mug in the sink. "I want some of that tomorrow." He pointed to the heating pot.

"I'll make sure it's ready," Jamie told him with a tired smile.

"Thanks for coming guys. We might make this an annual thing."

"We all need family," Jamie said quietly, pressing into Chris' throat before facing forward again.

"Go pour him into bed. He looks ready to pass out," Ed said, smiling at Jamie.

Jamie yawned hugely. "I already did twenty minutes ago. This is all a hologram."

Even Duncan laughed at that. Ed went to gather their coats from the spare bedroom.

"Thanks for having me," Ed heard Duncan say as he neared with the jackets.

"Glad you could come. Be here in the morning. There's no way the two of us can eat all the food that's still left."

"I will certainly help anyway I can," Duncan offered.

"Then you're hired," Chris agreed. He walked both Ed and Duncan to the front door. "Drive careful."

"Night," Ed called walking away. Duncan did the same then trotted to catch up to Ed.

* * * *

Duncan was on Ed's heels when he opened the front door. His hand was warm riding in the sexy man's rear pocket, and had been there since they'd gotten out of the Jeep. Every step twitched tight skin against his palm, making Duncan want to squeeze in ownership.

After an entire evening either in Ed's arms, or close to it, Duncan wanted to get naked. Needed to feel hot skin, feverish kisses, and hear Ed's deep growls of pleasure. Ed had driven him silently crazy all night. It had started on the hayride with the simple contact, then the kisses that had rocked his world because he couldn't tear Ed's clothes off right that second. Duncan had showed restraint, but now… Now Ed was his.

The door swung inward allowing them to enter the dim living room and he followed without hesitation.

"Does Margo need to go out?"

Duncan spotted her curled up in the corner she seemed to have claimed since her first visit. "She's out cold." Her nose didn't even quiver at their entrance. "Lock the door," Duncan said against Ed's ear.

"Mmm. Yeah?"

Duncan flexed his fingers, capturing more muscle through denim. "Definitely." He wasn't sure he was any closer to unknotting the mess he'd arrived in Silo with that evening. When he was staring into those brown eyes, there wasn't much of anything he wanted to think about. The questions that had plagued him had taken a backseat to more pressing demands. Nothing was going to miraculously pop up and provide answers between that moment and the next morning. Not explanations for the friends-only distance Ed had first shown, or the kisses that had set fire to the night, or even the few words that he'd let slip past his own lips.

There was *right now*. If Ed's tremors were any indication, Duncan wasn't alone in wanting the same thing.

Reluctantly, he had to release that wonderful handful to remove jackets. Then he was glued to Ed, corralling him toward the bedroom. His hand had somehow found its place right back in that pocket with his other arm clutched around Ed's midsection, with him pressed firmly into Duncan's chest.

Once they cleared the doorway, Duncan didn't waste a minute, grasping the sweater and jerking it upward. "Off," he demanded. "Need you."

Ed's breathing hitched then sped up, but the garment was swept off in a heartbeat, exposing a broad frame and shoulders that Duncan wanted to lick.

Ed took Duncan by surprise when he whirled and captured his face in warm palms, slamming his mouth over Duncan's.

Duncan rocked on his heels, his world tipping precariously for several seconds as blood pulsed and raged through his body. Duncan gave in and leaned into Ed's strength, nudging him toward the bed. With a hooked leg behind a knee, he knocked them both flat, bouncing to settle over Ed's broader width. The man was a rock. Duncan couldn't get enough of that.

He yanked his mouth free to take a deep breath. "I served with guys who worked for hours at a time to have a body like this."

"Did they turn you on?" Ed asked, grinding upward groin to groin.

A clamped palm captured him by the butt to hold him in place. Duncan moaned. He finally found words to answer. "No. Too many were conceited asswipes."

Ed snickered and Duncan took the opening, kissing him back with the same full-throttle force Ed had used on him seconds ago.

The scratch of seeking, calloused fingers dug under the sweater he wore and worked it up over his shoulders. Duncan had to let him go long enough to have it tugged free and tossed to the side. Cooler air tightened skin and each inhale and shift dragged sensitive buds over skin and wisps of hair. The visible fact his arm was completely exposed never even flicked into his consciousness. It had ceased to matter to Duncan because it had never mattered at all to Ed.

"Feel like a fucking god," Duncan said, hungry for the playground waiting for him. Hard chest, broad pecs, and muscles that rippled with each breath. Duncan nipped and sucked at Ed's jaw, being careful to not mark him until he was below the collar line, then he was open territory.

That was when the growling started. The fine hairs on Duncan's neck stood up in answer. *That* was the sound he longed for. Lost in passion, lost to the pain, and the pleasure. He lapped, bit, gnawed, and sucked, paying special attention to the protruding nips exposed to the air and Duncan's teeth. They tasted so good.

Gliding southward, he dragged loosened jeans away, purposely licking across the lines of Ed's abdominals. Wrangling jeans and drawers down over his rump and hips, Duncan slid down to the floor between Ed's thick thighs. The flex of those muscles made him lightheaded. Each one rocked the cock waiting for him.

The rush of hunger almost knocked him on his ass. He had to feel all of Ed, all that strength, the heat of his need.

Always. The one word thundered between his ears with the force of a crashing wave on rocks.

He swallowed, his vision blurring for a heartbeat.

"You okay down there?"

The note of valid concern yanked Duncan to the moment, to Ed's bedroom. A brown-eyed gaze landed on him.

"I'm okay. Not what you think."

Worry made Ed go still. "I'd hate to think I brought it on."

"Oh, man. Never you. Never you," he whispered, climbing unsteadily back up Ed's elongated length to cover him chest to chest. The reality was, Duncan was beginning to suspect Ed was his island, his rock in the wild seas of life.

And it terrified him. Now he knew what he'd been feeling for the last month. Why he'd all but begged Ed to stay. He knew he wasn't ready for *that*.

To hide the roiling morass seething inside, he lowered and staked a claim to the incredible, delicious lips patiently waiting for him.

This he could do without thinking twice. Sex. This had always been easy. It was carnal pleasures. The heat of the moment. Emotions *weren't* supposed to part of it. Neither was gut-clenching need.

He devoured Ed, sucking on lips and tongue fighting down the panic.

Don't leave.

Holy fucking shit. Fear sliced down his middle, battling the raging inferno of lusting hunger for supremacy of his attention. He didn't know how it had gotten to this point. The surge clawed at him, determined to suck him under, then Ed's hands gripped him, grounded him, and everything but the man skin to skin with him in that bed faded away.

Chapter Twenty-One

Ed tugged on Duncan, kicking off shoes at the same time. Then a wiggle and a leg hike and he was out of his jeans. He gasped, trying to breathe beneath the man's onslaught. He was voracious, keeping Ed guessing and incapable of thought with those kisses. Once on the bed, he maneuvered Duncan to finally reach his waist and divest his jeans and get the man equally naked.

It seemed no matter how hard he'd fought it, Duncan managed to worm his way back into Ed's core, picking at him and his desires until he snapped. Right that moment, he didn't care one blink who fucked who. He *needed*. He was so fucking horny after the night they'd spent, skin stretched until he thought he'd burst with the aching need Duncan caused.

A date. That's all it was supposed to be. Company to not go alone to the Christmas party. Duncan turned it into torture from the hayride onward. Hell, starting with the kiss under the mistletoe! He'd curled Ed's toes! Even when they'd been standing in the kitchen hanging out and talking, Duncan had been doing this little hip roll motion against Ed's dick that had kept him hard all...night...long. And Duncan had kept his word. Every single mistletoe branch they came under, he took blatant advantage. Some had been power kisses, sensual knee-stoppers, or playful pursed pecked kisses. Ed had loved every one.

They still needed to talk. Eventually. Right now, they needed to fuck or he was going to explode. Ed was dying. His flesh felt on fire with the raging river of need burning from the inside to get outside. Duncan made him feel like such an animal. He liked the roughness underneath Duncan's exterior, that rebellious edge that slipped out when they were together. He had absolutely no clue if Duncan knew how to take it slow. The man embodied raw passion.

It melted Ed every time.

He moaned with Duncan's fierce kisses scattering his thoughts to the four corners. Thrusts of his tongue scraped his teeth. Duncan's hand was everywhere, from the top of his head to grasp at hair like he wanted to ride Ed into the sunset, down his chest until he gripped Ed's cock, fisting it like a crank.

"Fuck," Ed groaned. "Shit, Duncan." His heart pounded into his ribs with explosive force at the strength in that hand. Then Duncan blew his mind. Smooth, supple leather rolled over his sac. "Fucking shit!" Ed stiffened, fighting the waves of pleasure before they overwhelmed him.

He shoved Duncan's hands away, gasping to breathe. "Stop. Gonna make me lose it."

Duncan's throaty chuckle vibrated the bed. "I'll have to save that for a later date. Not yet."

While Ed caught his breath, Duncan rolled from the bed to finish stripping, tossing his shoes to land in his wadded jeans. "How do you want it tonight?"

Ed cried out when teeth snagged the sensitive loose skin of his sac. He felt branded. "Don't care." He really didn't.

The brush of air cooled him when Duncan's heat vanished. The sound of the drawer opening and closing told him what Duncan was doing. Then he was back on the bed.

Ed was already soaring, craving, and Duncan had to push him that much harder. The heat of his mouth was a furnace when Duncan engulfed the end of Ed's cock. He jerked, clutching the blankets in trembling fists. "Not going to last," he whined.

"Yes, you are."

The cool control in Duncan's voice drove him crazy. Then he ringed his sac with unyielding fingers and held him there, swollen and untouched, all the while he lavished Ed's hard length with a taunting tongue.

Tremors rocked his body, making the bed vibrate beneath them. Ed hungered for more of Duncan's sucking mouth until he was biting his knuckles fighting the whimpers and the screams of pleasure ripping through him.

"Oh, fuck," he panted when Duncan released him with a final stroke of his tongue. Ed felt like he'd been swimming underwater for days as he fought for every heaved breath.

"Over. Don't come yet."

Ed was shaking, but he managed to bring his body around. The wet press of two fingers was purely unapologetic as Duncan amped the energy.

"Just tell me if it's too much," he said.

Ed shook his head. He was wound so tight, he barely felt anything.

"Fuck me, sexy. That ass wants me, doesn't it?" The drive of fingers opened him up, spreading his entrance right before Duncan crooked a finger and found the bundle of nerves that set Ed on fire.

"Duncan!" Ed howled into his pillow, shaking his head. More pressure and the bite of pain that was so close to pleasure.

"Almost there."

Ed was losing it. His head was about to explode. The race of blood through his body raged like a machine, thunderous in its roar.

There was the shortest interruption. Sounds that weren't Ed dying from overstimulation filled in the blanks. Then there wasn't any warning, a single second of smooth flesh knocking at his backdoor, and then Duncan was pushing forward.

Duncan moaned, a guttural sound that filled every space of the room. "That is so good," he groaned. "Love that you can take it all."

Ed rocked, driving himself into Duncan's hip thrusts. It felt like Duncan could touch every inch, find every nerve. Ed panted, gasping out Duncan's name. Skin meeting skin was intoxicating as Duncan drove them higher, right up to the edge of the cliff.

Fingers dug into his hip, clawed at him. The heat of the room multiplied, surrounding them. Sparks split his vision. "Duncan!"

He jerked away. "Over! Now!"

The growly demand stroked Ed's needs, bombarding his nerves until he shivered with the relentless desire to come.

Duncan fit himself right between his spread thighs. "Hang on, baby," he offered, choked and gasping himself.

Ed's body opened for him and on a single slamming surge, Ed was filled to the hilt. His head snapped backward on his neck and he cried out. Duncan's full-throttle claiming ground over his prostate, leaving him breathless all over again.

"Fucking amazing," Duncan managed on harsh exhales.

His hair had swept over his face, obscuring nearly half. The single dark eye, the grimace of control edged by pleasure, the flushed tone of his skin. He was an animal, but never more beautiful. Ed became captured by his stare, pinned by the heat in them, by the strength of his body. Duncan's plunges began to stutter.

"Come with me. Need to feel you."

Ed's orgasm took less time to erupt than it took to understand Duncan's words. Contact was all it took, a firm heated palm and less than a half-dozen strokes. He was wired, powering through the bursts of release and then Duncan was there. Snarls, gasps, and staggered, choked attempts at breathing when lungs refused to reignite. With muscles pulsing in the aftermath, he slowly melted into the bed. Overheated skin rippled where they touched, damp and sticky.

Almost as though he feared one of them would break, Duncan eased away then sank forward, chest to chest. Both were sucking air like freight trains in the night. Duncan had officially scrambled his brain. He couldn't think. Speaking was an impossibility. It was a toss-up between passing out completely or simply floating in the between space of conscious and unconscious. It was a wonderful place to be. Shifting enough to touch, he brushed lips to skin and soaked up the all over reaction he got for it in return.

One arm rose and curled around Ed's head on the pillow, fingers threading through hair to caress.

Duncan blanketed Ed's body with his chin pressed into the crook of Ed's neck and shoulder. Even for the months they'd been seeing each other, nothing had ever come close to what they'd just shared.

As their breathing eased, Duncan fidgeted. "Be right back." He bussed a tender kiss to a collar bone before hefting himself upward. Duncan returned with a damp cloth and a towel. Cleaning up, Ed sighed when gentle strokes recreated crackles beneath skin, nerves that were still sensitive.

When he finished, Duncan took it all to the bathroom. After a few minutes, with his one arm now bare, he urged Ed off the blanket and sheets. It was like fitting into the most perfect coat, the way he nestled body to body against Duncan.

There were a lot of thoughts in the outer reaches of his mind, but right then, about the only thing he could focus on was the heat generated between them, the soothing kind that would rock them both to sleep.

Ed opened his mouth, his lashes fluttering for several shocked heartbeats when the words almost tripped off his tongue. Catching himself at the last possible moment before utter catastrophe, he bit his lip, and instead brought Duncan closer hiding his almost blunder. There was still so much left unsaid. All those things he couldn't bring his brain online to think about at the moment. Worries that went beyond himself, as well.

"Relax, sexy," Duncan crooned. Warm kisses were gentle along his nape, comforting.

"Will you still be here in the morning?"

Duncan tensed, then sagged onto the pillow. "Go to sleep."

Almost with the clarity of second sight, Ed knew that had been Duncan's intention. To vanish before morning light. Ed wasn't the only one who'd had his world tilted and ripped in two. Everything Duncan had done had confused him. He didn't need more head games. Not now, not after what was said, or after what they'd just shared. "Will you still be here?"

"I'll be here," Duncan finally conceded, though it took long enough that Ed had to believe it hadn't been his intent after tonight. He'd been poised to run.

Ed didn't push. Both were on shaky ground, but after almost letting his real feelings slip free, feelings he hadn't fully realized until that moment, he needed some kind of understanding of himself, for himself, and his heart. He needed time.

He'd fought it all along to keep his heart from being broken. Now, it would be devastating to say the words and have Duncan refuse him, or vanish. Evening his breathing to sleep, he held it all close, wrapped up and behind a steel door. The man in his bed was the real deal. The best he could do was take it one day at a time.

There was still his mother, his parents' pending move, his job, friends. No one thing held enough weight to determine his future.

No one thing there in *Silo*.

However, Duncan could change everything with a few simple and honest words. If he was brave enough to love Ed. If he was strong enough to be vulnerable. If he was willing to let Ed love him in return. If this was more than sex. Ed had thought after tonight it might have been. It was there in the man's kisses, in his touch. Ed knew he had to feel something, but he also knew trying too hard to get Duncan to open up would only drive him away.

The doubts swirled and weaved through his mind as sleep drew him under. It took longer than usual to find that perfect restful slope, even with Duncan's strength and heat wrapped around him.

Duncan had given his word, yet Ed feared come morning he'd find himself alone in the bed. Stroking the hand that held him with light fingers until he could fall asleep, he kept the contact as proof that he wasn't alone. Not yet.

Chapter Twenty-Two

Ed blinked as gray morning light beat against his eyelids. The warmth of the bed called to him to indulge in more sleep, but something else had awakened him. He knew what it was before he even opened his eyes. Shifting the other way where Duncan had slept, he wanted to rage. The bed was empty. He was alone. Instead of cursing like a madman, he buried his head into the pillow and punched the bed. He'd expected it, but the shock of it still gutted him down the middle with the dull icy pain of an icicle stabbing him over and over.

"God damn it!" He growled and snarled. He knew this would happen. He'd *known* Duncan had lied. Ed had known it last night, he'd heard it in his voice, felt it in the tense hold of his arms. That burned even more than finding him gone. He was trying to believe in the man. This wasn't helping.

Fighting the disappointment, he gusted a breath and flipped to his back. The gray dawn light seemed extremely weak. Facing the window, he noted it was snowing. That explained a lot. The snowfall wasn't thick, but heavy winter clouds blocked a lot of light.

He needed to get moving. Regardless of being alone or not, Chris and Jamie were expecting him. Lying in bed, he chewed on his lip, watching the snow fall. It kind of matched his mood. Thick, heavy, and gray.

The barely audible click of the front door several minutes later was followed by the rustle of clothes, feet, and paws. "Shh. Lay down."

Ed froze immediately before he wanted to disappear into the bed. *Oh, fuck.* Duncan hadn't left. Searching the bedroom quickly, he didn't see Duncan's attachment or protective arm sheath. The man was a ninja.

"Hey, you're awake." Unsure hazel eyes studied him from the bedroom doorway.

Ed crawled upward on the bed, patting the covers over his lower body. "I didn't hear you get up."

Duncan swallowed. "You sleep like a rock, man," he said, offhandedly. "Threw a party and you didn't budge."

Ed smiled softly. He was in his own bed. He slept better. Apparently so well, he never heard Duncan moving around or dressing. And by the hint of guilt coloring his face, Ed was positive he'd been as quiet as a church mouse. Made him wonder just how quiet Duncan had been to have heard absolutely *nothing*. He wasn't going to demand an explanation. Duncan was there and that was all that mattered. "I bet you're cold."

"Some."

He glimpsed the clock. It was barely eight. "We have time. Come warm up."

Duncan's shoulders rose and fell with a deep inhale. Ed didn't comment when Duncan stripped out of everything—again. Didn't mention that he wore his attachment. Facts were facts. He'd planned on leaving, but something had kept him from getting in his truck and vanishing, likely forever.

When winter-chilled skin slid into the bed and found his, Ed shivered. "Brr."

Duncan smiled, snuggling to hide in Ed's chest. "I gave Margo water and some food I keep stashed in the truck."

Ed didn't push, accepting his reasoning. He'd put on a lot of clothing to dash to his truck. "Get closer. You're a damn ice cube."

Duncan stroked his hand over Ed's chest. "It's a balmy twenty-seven. It's nearly summer."

Ed snickered and hunkered down, tucking the sheets around them to warm icy skin. "Almost swimming weather."

Duncan burrowed into him, soft laughter rumbling between them. A leg moved and almost by habit, they wound together, looping and bending until they naturally locked hip to hip. The silence grew, a languorous drifting that was easy for the both of them. Slowly, the occasional shiver that crossed Duncan's frame ceased.

Ed sifted fingers into Duncan's snow-dampened hair. "So... We're okay?"

Resting on a shoulder, Duncan raised enough to meet Ed's gaze. "Not a fucking clue what I'm doing, but yeah, we're good."

Ed really wondered what had made him change his mind, what had kept him there, but didn't want to ruin the moment with his own fears and needs to know. Duncan would be gone in a flash if he poked too hard. For now, this was perfect. Maybe when Duncan was ready, he'd explain it.

He protected himself in silence. Ed could respect that. So long as he didn't box Ed out completely, he could take what Duncan dished out as a work in progress.

* * * *

The second Duncan found Ed awake, he knew he'd been stone-cold busted. He'd even gone so far as to put Margo in her cage and get behind the wheel. Then he'd raised his chin and stared hard at that front door through a snow-dusted windshield, and felt like the biggest asshole for cutting out and running. He wasn't a hypocrite, but if he started that engine, he'd be that and worse. He'd never gone back on his word. Never.

Duncan was the one to paint himself into this corner. No one else.

He'd cursed under his breath, reversed his trip and brought a confused Margo inside, remembering at the last second before he opened the door to actually grab her stock bag so she could eat.

Buried under the blanket and hiding in the crook of Ed's neck, muscles relaxed as he warmed up again. Ed stroked his side with a lazy thumb, no pressure, just...cuddling? He grumbled softly. "You're ruining my image," he groused.

"I am?"

"No one gets to know I cuddle. Deal?" Duncan didn't have a soft bone in his body. There was absolutely nothing *cuddly* about him. Well, nothing except for Ed, apparently. He refused to admit he was enjoying this. No way.

"Oh?" Now Ed sounded humored. "And what do I get for keeping this golden secret?"

"You take it to your grave and I won't tell anyone you keep a stash of Snickers in the freezer."

"Hey!" Ed grunted. He went contemplatively silent, then, "Okay. Deal."

Duncan grinned because he knew Ed had let him off easy. If Snickers minis were Ed's largest vice, he could live with that.

Duncan's eyelids were low, his breathing even. It simply felt *good* where he was.

"I'm beginning to think you really meant what you said." Ed's voice held a contented, rumbled sound.

Duncan wasn't going to play dumb. He couldn't pretend he hadn't said those words last night. His heart rate sped up a notch. "Just... Give me time." There was more than one thing he'd never done before. Exposing his heart, to anyone, was one of them.

"If you're honest with me, I can give you all the time that exists." Ed's warm lips coasted from his temple to the corner of his mouth. "Don't run without giving us a chance. Talk to me first, okay?"

Duncan stiffened for a split second then sagged into Ed's warmth. *Totally busted.* "It's hard to do that."

"I know." Ed shifted down on the bed to curl around Duncan more.

Ed teased at the corner of Duncan's mouth with the tip of his tongue, dropping soft touches until Duncan lifted his chin enough to receive his kiss. A hand cupped the back of his head and massaged his scalp, sending rippling shivers down Duncan's neck and spine.

Duncan put a hand on Ed's chest and pushed. The man didn't so much as rock. The press of an evil grin burned his jaw. Before Duncan could argue, those massaging fingers fisted his hair and arched his head on his neck, baring his throat for roving teeth and taunting lips. Slow strokes over his pulse drowned him in sensation. Instead of pushing at Ed, he clutched at his hip, bringing him closer.

The urge to roll Ed over and take control was strong, but Ed wasn't relenting. He wasn't pinning Duncan so much as simply not giving in to his demands, and with each passing second, Duncan's focus faded until every nerve was awake and begging for Ed's mouth.

Ed moved with unfazed patience. Found spots and pockets that powered blood through Duncan's veins, caresses that made him ache. A whimper escaped and Duncan's toes curled.

"Want you."

Duncan flinched. It wasn't conscious. "I…" He swallowed.

"Shh. Not right now. Relax. Going to love you, feel you." Ed raised above him enough to stare him right in the eye. "I want you to think about how good everything feels. That's all you have to do. Feel." Ed studied him. The hand buried in Duncan's hair slid free to stroke his face and jaw.

Duncan bit his lip. He could see so much in those brown eyes. He nodded, unable to put his thoughts to voice. He wasn't exactly sure what he would say.

"One thing at a time," Ed replied. A promise.

Duncan waited for the explosive passion, for the wrestle of carnal pleasure. Ed's movements were slow and methodical, focused on Duncan, meant to calculatingly melt him. Kisses and touches. Fingers and lips. He was left gripping at Ed or the bedding as Ed sucked on Duncan's nipples. Duncan had lovers who'd paid him attention, but there was something stronger in Ed's actions. Something deliberate. Something unselfish. Duncan felt it as he began to succumb to the spell. It had never been in his nature to surrender, but right that moment, whatever and everything Ed was doing, was coaxing him into it naturally.

There was no fear over losing control to the man worshiping his body. He could stop Ed with a breath, or a word. There was something so very freeing in that knowledge because he didn't *want* to stop him. He stretched his spine offering—begging for more— and Ed ran with it.

Duncan moaned, his throat raw as his breathing grew ragged when Ed closed his mouth around the tip of Duncan's dick. "Fucking Christ. Yeah, that… Oh, shit. Ed."

Ed hummed, clearly enjoying what he was doing. The vibrations showered sparks across Duncan's chest, making his skin prickle. The slick heat of tongue drove him insane when Ed curled and rolled around the shaft.

A tremor, a wince of apprehension tightened his throat as a cool, damp finger stroked over his entrance. Ed hummed again, taking a few more inches between his lips, distracting Duncan.

When that finger returned, he sucked at the same time and Duncan almost howled at the combination. Ed teased, rimmed, stroked, and pressed but never breached. Propped over Duncan, he raised his gaze and silently asked.

Duncan wet dry lips and nodded. He had to know if he could do this. Only… Ed didn't do anything. He continued the oral assault on his cock, bobbing, sucking and licking in such a way, Duncan wouldn't have been surprised to see his dick come out knotted like a cherry stem.

Gradually, the anticipation, the worry, and anxiety faded. Pleasure reigned. Duncan pushed downward seeking the firm thrust of pressure that was just out of reach and gasped as his body opened up.

Stars streaked through his vision. He didn't refuse it. Didn't reject Ed. Fuck, Ed was making him seek the pleasure, hunt for the twitch and thrust of his touch. The wet sensation increased. Lube. He had no idea when Ed had grabbed it, but it was adding another layer of discovery. The darkest, innate fears he carried forever didn't materialize. If it was because it was Ed, because of the way he touched Duncan, he honestly didn't know. One of the ugliest walls in his mind slowly crumbled beneath Ed's tender loving.

He cried out Ed's name, disbelief rolling through him as powerful shocks rocketed upward. He surged downward hunting for more, to feel more. Ed gave it to him, filling him in centimeters while sucking on his cock with enough force to drain his balls.

"Shit." Duncan whimpered. "Yes." His world was tipping. He knew he was skipping on the edge.

"One more thing for right now," Ed rasped.

Duncan clutched at the bedding, his senses in overload. It was the smallest thing, but it almost killed Duncan. That bundle of nerves Duncan had taken for granted when it came to pleasuring his partners.

Ed found it at the same instant he drew on Duncan's cock, sucking him wildly, riding him with abandon between lips that were stretched around the girth. Duncan managed one snuck peek of that gorgeous man and lost it.

Ed grunted, encouraging him through to the end. He throbbed all the way down his spine. Duncan's sac clenched, jetting out rope after rope of seed for Ed to devour. Slowly, the thick heat of the finger filling his ass withdrew, sending Duncan for another loop.

He didn't want to let him go. He hadn't anticipated that.

Gasping desperately for oxygen, he swung an arm over his eyes. "Fucking shit. What did you do?"

Ed's chuckle was hoarsely graveled. "Made love to you," he answered, coming to rest beside Duncan's head on the pillow, panting shallowly. The smile Duncan couldn't see was clear in his voice.

"But..." Duncan didn't get it. "You... You didn't..." He couldn't put his thoughts into words. He wasn't even sure his body was still attached as hard as he'd come. He was floating somewhere over his body from the endorphin rush.

"I got everything I wanted out of it," Ed told him gently. He began to stroke circles on Duncan's stomach. "It's not always about coming. Sometimes, it's just about making the person feel special." A gentle kiss warmed his shoulder. "Sometimes, it's about showing how you feel." A firm exhale bathed skin. "Does that scare you?"

Duncan maneuvered a weightless hand under Ed's frame and brought him close with a cupped palm. "No," he finally admitted when he could breathe deep enough to speak. His lips brushed Ed's temple.

It didn't.

There was hope for him yet.

Epilogue

"This is the last box, Dad." Ed stacked it in the moving van on the padded furniture at the end, then jumped from the doorway to the driveway. He and Duncan closed the doors. Kent snapped the lock into place.

"Okay. Let me get them going." Kent walked to the front of the moving company rig to talk with the drivers. His mother was sitting on a folding patio chair that they could throw in the car, watching the neighborhood go by. She was smiling and seemed settled with the idea of the move. Her health was stable and she was fairly cognizant of her surroundings. Her ability to function at a near pre-stroke level had eased a lot of the stress for Ed over the last months.

Harsh snows in February delayed his parents' plans to mid-April, but he has glad for it more than he wanted to let his parents see. The idea of them doing what had to be done in the briskness of dead winter hadn't sat well with him.

While he had a minute, he turned to Duncan, both moving out of the van's way, to lean against his dad's car. "Now, you're positive you and Margo will be okay in Silo?"

Duncan rolled his eyes. "You and your Dad. That gene is genetic."

Ed furrowed his brow, then… "Smartass." Ed wound a hand behind his head and drew him close.

"It was your idea to move us all at the same time."

Duncan *had* to remind him of that fact. "Just pick me up at the airport on Saturday, will ya?"

"Get your ass to the airport, and I'll think about it."

Ed's lips twitched then shaking his head, he gave in to the grin. "I'll call tonight and when we get to Florida." Ed was pretty sure he'd be calling more often than that. Since Christmas, it was growing harder and harder to be apart from the man in his arms.

Long weeks at the fire station had seemed endless with Duncan at his own home and not in Silo. Phone calls hadn't cut it. His impatience to finally have Duncan with him had scattered his ability to plan properly. Thus the ill-timed moves of two households. He'd miscommunicated with his dad and wound up moving them the weekend after Duncan had moved to Silo. And then as soon as he was getting home at the end of the week, they were going to move out of the garage apartment. His place was simply too small for two full grown men and a dog. So three moves in less than fourteen days.

But it would all be worth it.

Duncan slipped his arms around Ed's waist. The light spring breezes flirted with Duncan's hair. He scooped it into his palm and held it away from his face. This thing between them hadn't been perfect or easy, but it was getting better. Stronger. Ed was patient. So long as Duncan didn't run, so long as he tried to talk, Ed could wait. Everything Duncan was inside was the man Ed needed in his life. Duncan was trying and that right there was the largest step, the strength he knew the man had inside to allow Ed *in*.

"Just tell me you're going to miss me," Ed whispered.

Duncan swallowed. "I will." His gaze danced around to make sure Kent was still otherwise occupied. "I'm not a romance guy."

"I think I caught that." Ed tickled at his nape with a thumbnail.

Duncan drew a slow breath. "Margo is going to mope like a wet sock until you get home."

"Just Margo?" he asked quietly.

"Maybe. Maybe not," Duncan allowed. He pushed lightly into Ed's stroking touch. "Tell me something."

"Sure." Ed leaned against the trunk of his dad's car, drawing Duncan with him.

"Why?"

"Why what?"

"Why…" Duncan shrugged. "Everything."

Ed's fingers caressed as he stared right into his eyes. "Because I love you."

Duncan chewed on his lip, digesting those words. "You've known for a while, haven't you?"

"Yes."

"And you're still here?"

Ed's chest expanded as he heard and saw more than just the spoken words. His heart even dared to flutter a little. "Told you, I'd give you all the time you needed. I knew it then. I knew you cared and for me, that's enough. When you're ready, I'm here."

"If I'm ready now?" Duncan said on a bare whisper.

"That's up to you. I'd love to hear it before I take off," Ed told him, almost jumping for joy to hear the exact opposite of one of his most silent fears. The fear that Duncan had convinced himself it would never happen had nagged at him ruthlessly at his lowest points. The man was stubborn in ways even a mule could learn. He urged him to tip on his neck, to peer into his face. Rugged and loved.

"You still terrify the fuck out of me, Edward Norwood."

Ed snorted. "You still frustrate the shit out of me. Yet, here we are."

"I guess so." Duncan straightened and licked his lip. "Your dad knew it all along, too."

"I think he did."

"Never thought I'd ever be called son."

Ed continued to caress and connect. "He appreciates you, and he cares for you. Mom I think understands, but she likes you just the same."

Duncan looked over his shoulder and they both spotted Ed's parents walking one last time into the house. A final goodbye for the next leg of this journey they would share together. The pulse in Duncan's neck skipped. He was trying to get it out and now the pressure was on.

He gulped, then swallowed twice more. "Never wanted this, never thought I'd be able to feel this."

"I know."

"So scared or not, huh?"

Ed held his breath. He wouldn't push, but... He could feel it. Right *there. Come on, sexy. Say it.*

Dark lashes fell flushed to Duncan's cheeks hiding enigmatic colors and all the thoughts swirling behind them. They opened with the intensity of sun-heated lasers. "I love you," he blurted in a mad rush. He gasped, heaving for oxygen before finally calming in marginal waves. "I love you." He smiled when it came even easier the second time around.

"And the sky didn't fall," Ed remarked.

"I knew you needed to hear it before you left," Duncan explained. His own fingers skated over Ed's shoulder. "And yes, I'll be here when you get back."

"You better be. You're my ride."

Duncan groaned, but laughed roughly through it.

"I'm putting Mom in the car." Kent walked up behind them with Judy on his arm.

"Okay, Dad," Ed answered. "You're the best thing that's ever happened to me, Duncan." He lifted strands of hair and let them slip through his fingers. "I plan on showing you how much as often as possible as soon as I get home."

"I'll be here."

And this time, Ed knew without a question, Duncan would be.

About the Author

Diana DeRicci is the sexy, flirty pen name of Diana Castilleja. A romance author at heart, DeRicci's writing takes you into a saucier spectrum of sensuality and sexual adventure, where a happily-ever-after is still the key to any story. Diana lives in central Texas with her husband, one son, and a feisty little Chihuahua named Rascal. You can catch the latest news on all of Diana DeRicci's writing and books on her website listed below. Feel free to drop Diana an e-mail. She'd love to hear from you.

Visit her online at:
www.DianaDeRicci.com

PURPLE SWORD PUBLICATIONS
Romantic Speculative Fiction
www.purplesword.com

www.ingramcontent.com/pod-product-compliance
Lightning Source LLC
Chambersburg PA
CBHW072110170626
46813CB00004B/1502